To The

DARK TOWER

"Listen to reason, Tom," the voice called. "You're fooling yourself if you think you can escape. The only way out of here is straight past me."

A ladle directly beneath them was slowly upended, and in a brief dazzle of light Tom saw that what the voice claimed was true. Jack himself was standing squarely in the wide exit from the mill. There was a second brilliant sunburst, and Tom also noted that more than one person had followed them up the chain. Several stealthy forms were now gliding between the girders, each with a glint of metal in one hand.

"I'll make a bargain with you, Tom," Jack called enticingly. "Give yourself up and your friends will come to no harm. You have my word on that."

A bargain, Jack called it, but what alternative was there? The only exit was blocked, and a ring of armed figures was closing in steadily.

Also by Victor Kelleher

Brother Night
Del-Del

and many other titles

To The
DARK TOWER

VICTOR KELLEHER

RED FOX

A Red Fox Book

Published by Random House Children's Books
20 Vauxhall Bridge Road, London SW1V 2SA

A division of Random House UK Ltd

London Melbourne Sydney Auckland
Johannesburg and agencies throughout
the world

© Victor Kelleher 1992

First published by Julia MacRae 1992
Red Fox edition 1994

3 5 7 9 10 8 6 4 2

Printed and bound in Great Britain by
Cox & Wyman Ltd, Reading, Berkshire

RANDOM HOUSE UK Limited Reg. No. 954009

ISBN 0 09 921141 6

Better this present than a past like that . . .

What in the midst lay but the Tower itself ?
  The round squat turret, blind as the fool's heart,
  Built of brown stone, without a counterpart
In the whole world.

Robert Browning,
  'Childe Roland to the Dark Tower Came'

1 It was like a door that had been left open invitingly.
On impulse he stepped through, and immediately
regretted it. He was standing in a gloomy low-ceilinged
cave, the walls carved out of solid ice, the atmosphere
so cold that his frozen breath billowed about his face.

There were others in there already, waiting, eight of them
huddled together in a corner, their eyes fixed hopefully on his.
They were dressed exactly as he was, in pale sheepskin jackets and trousers, with matching boots, and caps pulled down
over their ears. Most, like him, were in their mid-teens; and
their faces, pinched as much by fear as by cold, seemed
strangely familiar, as though he had known them all his life.
One, a girl with intense dark eyes, nodded towards the end of
the room. When he failed to respond, she nodded again, more
urgently than before, her lips forming words soundlessly.

He saw then what he should have noticed earlier: a second
door set low in the end wall. It was much smaller and far less
enticing than the first, yet he felt drawn to it just the same. Or
was he merely being urged on by his silent companions?
Another of them, a tall burly figure, gave him a smile of
encouragement which was instantly reflected in all the other
faces. He found it difficult to resist, as if this, after all, was why
he was here: to help them in their mysterious venture. And
under the pressure of their combined appeal, he ducked down
and crawled through the low opening.

This time he emerged onto a windswept ledge. Above him,
murky grey clouds raced across an even greyer sky. Below –
far below – lay a desolate valley heaped with tumbled slabs of
ice. There was no sign of life anywhere, and if the cave had
been cold, this was far worse. Already his face and heavily

1

mittened hands were growing numb, and each intake of breath was like a knife probing his chest. He shivered, from more than just the freezing temperature, and hunched down, determined to go no further.

Instantly the girl with the dark eyes was there on the ledge beside him, her mouth working soundlessly once again. Raising one arm, she pointed straight across the valley, to yet another door, this one set into the opposite cliff-face, its heavy wooden timbers clotted with ice and snow.

Oddly, he wasn't surprised to find it there. He might almost have been the one showing it to her; his arm, not hers, now raised and pointing.

"That could be the place," he said aloud, voicing the words on her lips, and she nodded, apparently instructed by him, and crawled back inside the cave.

Despite the desolation of the valley, he was relieved once she had gone. There was something unsettling about her presence that he could not quite pin down. Also, he understood somehow that the rest was for him to do alone. His special task. And after tightening the straps of his back-pack, he squirmed out over the edge and began the descent.

This part at least was straightforward, something he was expert at. His booted feet searched for and found the toe-holds he needed; his mittened fingers slipped easily into the tiny cracks and crevices that scarred the sheer surface. With the wind soughing drearily past his cheeks, he inched his way down, and would have reached the valley floor without incident had it not been for the sudden jolt. Not only the cliff-face moved. The rest of the valley, even the racing clouds, seemed to tilt sideways. For a few seconds everything grew blurred, as if about to dissolve. Then, just as abruptly, the surrounding world moved back into focus and the cliff steadied beneath his hands.

After that he was glad enough to reach the valley. He felt safer there – for a while anyway – but when he was only half-way across, that same jolting action recurred. He was trudging past a towering slab of ice, and all at once the ground shuddered and threatened to collapse. Immediately overhead there was an ominous cracking noise, and he threw himself down, his whole body braced for the expected impact.

An impact that never came. There was a cry high on the

wind – it might almost have been the wind itself – and when he raised his head the towering slab, the chaos all about him, lay undisturbed. In the whole dreary scene he could detect only one small change. Up on the ledge, where two of his companions had emerged from the cave. The burlier of the two called again, a wordless bird-like sound, felt rather than heard, that conveyed feelings of warmth, of friendliness. The smaller, dark-eyed figure, silent as ever, merely waved him on.

Obediently, he approached the opposite wall and paused. Behind him the two figures remained watching from the ledge, as if trying to impose their own stillness on the valley. Conscious of those dark eyes following his every move, he began the slow climb upwards. He was wary now, expecting at any moment to feel the earth tremble, the sky to wheel above his head; but minutes passed and the cliff remained rock-steady. Apart from his own slow progress, the only movement was in the scudding clouds and the chill breeze that froze the sweat on his forehead.

He looked up and saw that he was nearly there. One more foothold, one more cautious step, and his hands curled safely over another narrow ledge. He clambered onto it, and the door was right before him, its iron bolt frozen solid, the upper part of the frame festooned with icicles. Unaccountably, the closeness of those weathered timbers filled him with excitement, as though at last he had reached the end of a long search. For a moment he forgot his companions on the opposite ledge. Glancing down, he noticed as though for the first time the coils of rope wound about his waist, and the small axe hanging from a loop on his jacket. Detaching the axe, he smashed the ice around the iron bolt. With almost reckless disregard he struck next at the row of icicles. They let out a high discordant chime as they broke free and clattered about his feet. The door itself gave way more grudgingly, and he had to chip at the ice along both jambs before he was able to force it open.

The room within looked as gloomy as the cavern he had just left. At one end stood an unused hearth, a heap of wood beside it. Attracted by the prospect of warmth, he was making for the wood when he stopped in mid-stride: for against one wall, on a low bed of bare planks, lay the naked body of a

3

man. He was very old, his limbs wasted and withered, his toothless mouth sunken in. Whether or not he was dead was difficult to tell, because like everything else he was frozen into immobility, his skin a bluish-grey and dusted with a gleaming film of frost.

The boy approached the body cautiously. Taking off his cap, he placed an ear against the pitifully thin chest and listened. Could he detect a faint heartbeat? Again it was difficult to tell, especially with his own nervous pulse thudding in his head. Better, he thought, to take no chances. Slipping off his back-pack, he found inside a bedroll of sheepskin which he wrapped securely about the ancient body. There was also a small tinderbox in the pack, ready for just such a moment as this. He struck a spark into the nest of tinder, and within minutes there was enough flame to transfer to the hearth. A few minutes more and he had the smoky beginnings of a fire.

As the first suggestion of warmth seeped into the room, he checked again on the old man. He lay as still as ever, his parchment-like skin brittle dry, his mouth gaping upon emptiness. Dead? the boy wondered, and was overtaken by a vague sense of having failed in some important task. Had he perhaps arrived too late? But from where? And too late for what?

He shook his head, baffled, and examined the old man's face more carefully. How old it was! How closed! Like a mask designed to hide or protect the person behind it. Wizened and empty of all expression, it told him nothing – the features, still brushed with frost, gradually receding into the dusk even as he watched.

Dusk! The boy looked around him, startled at how shadowy and indistinct the room had grown. The day, it seemed, had slipped away unnoticed. Across the valley his companions would be waiting impatiently. Yes, if he closed his eyes and concentrated, he could feel them calling, pleading for him to return.

As if to underscore the urgency of those silent voices, the room tilted sharply. Swam out of focus. The shadows parted, like a door opening onto a lighted corridor, and then closed again. He was left in near darkness, the gloom broken only by a glimmer of fire from the hearth.

Realising that there was not much time left, he heaped the

4

fire with logs and groped his way over to the door and out onto the ledge. The twilight and the wind greeted him icily. With half-numb fingers he uncoiled the rope from about his waist, secured one end to the door-jamb, and tossed the free end down into the obscurity of the valley.

"We're coming!" the silent voices were assuring him. "Coming!"

Dimly, against the opposite cliff-face, he could just detect his companions. Eight dark shapes, all in a row, they were swarming down another rope. One after the other, like fragments of the advancing night, they flitted across the valley floor and up towards him. He counted them as they clambered onto the ledge and entered the room: . . . four . . . five . . . six . . . seven . . . The last and smallest of the figures, the girl with dark, intense eyes, was struggling somewhere below. He could hear her gasping breaths, her groaning effort as she fought the rope.

"Wait!" he called out and swung down to help her.

She shook her head angrily and tried to push him off, but he had already caught her hand in his. She weighed much less than he had expected. Hardly more than his young brother who . . .

Brother?

The sky reeled and cracked. The cliff buckled and swelled outwards. In a jagged lightning flash, he saw her face clearly, her eyes dark with resentment. Accusation. Somewhere far off, in another place, he heard a faint cry. A familiar name spoken aloud. He would have answered, out of habit as much as need, but the sky had steadied, the darkness had closed around him. And he and the girl were lying on the ledge together, her frail body quivering like a bird's.

He did not follow her into the room straight away. Some instinct warned him to hold back. Slowly he gathered in the rope and wound it about his waist. The sky was totally black now. Unnaturally so. Cloudless, moonless, starless. But how could that be? He lifted his head suspiciously. Surely . . .

Before he could formulate the thought, the door opened wide, as invitingly as that other door, right at the beginning. Moved by the same impulse (urged on by the same voices?) he walked through.

Not into the cold, gloomy room he had left. The fire was

now roaring in the hearth, its flickering light patterning the ceiling. Gone was the freezing atmosphere, the air warm and inviting. Gone, too, was the body of the old man. On the low bed where he had lain, all that remained was a loose crumple of sheepskin. Gathered around the bed were the boy's eight companions, their faces no longer pale, but glowing in the firelight. Such strange faces! Almost elfin in shape, fine-boned and pointed at the chin. They turned towards him, laughing, welcoming, all fear gone from their eyes.

"But he's dead!" he wanted to tell them, remembering the frosted skin, the sunken mouth. "I arrived . . . no, I was summoned too late."

They shook their heads in denial, mouths thrown open in silent laughter. The tallest of them, the burly figure, reached down and peeled back a layer of sheepskin: to reveal another face, smooth and unlined; a tiny pinkish body. The boy blinked and looked again, but there was no mistake. A sleeping child lay curled up within the warm folds, its temples delicately veined, its head crowned with a fluff of golden hair. Tenderly, the big hands of the companion scooped the child up, drew the sheepskin back around it until only the sleeping face could be seen. A face both closed and beautiful in repose. Those same hands held the child out towards the boy. Offered it to him as if it were a precious gift.

He was about to accept it when the dark-eyed girl snatched the bundle and pressed it greedily to her breast. "Mine!" her eyes seemed to tell him. Out of all those present, her face alone was untouched by laughter, her expression as resentful and accusing as when he had rescued her below the ledge.

From under their feet there came a rumbled warning, the fire flaring up briefly, and her burly companion placed an arresting hand on her shoulder. She flinched guiltily, like someone caught in the act of stealing, and relaxed her hold on the child. Reluctantly, her face half-averted, she held the bundle out before her, mouthing words as she did so.

The boy, reading her lips, managed to decipher the first part of her message.

"You are the . . ."

"What?" he asked quickly. "What am I?" Because all at once it was vitally important that he understand.

His own outstretched hands were already slipping beneath

6

the child when she mouthed the words again. And this time he followed every word.

"You are the . . ."

But the sudden weight of the child made him lurch forward. He clutched at it, hèld it fast. At the same moment there was a sharp report from the earth beneath him, and the sky, the cliff, the room split in two, dissolved, as a blinding light came pouring in.

2 There was a swish of curtains and the fresh light of morning came pouring in. His mother was standing over by the window, glaring at him, her greying hair falling in wisps about a face prematurely lined by care.

"What are you playing at, Tom?" she said angrily. "I've been calling you this past hour. Don't pretend you didn't hear me."

The bed bounced and sagged and his young brother, Denny, leaned over him, laughing.

"You should have seen yourself," he said, his babyish cheeks bunching up into a grin. "You were making noises and twitching, just like Rusty next door, when he dreams he's chasing rabbits."

"Rabbits?"

Tom rose groggily, his head thick with sleep, and swung his legs out of bed. The shock of the cold lino on his bare feet brought with it a shred of memory.

"Not old . . ." he mumbled. "Only a child when I . . ."

"A child in years, maybe," his mother cut in sharply, "but with a man's responsibilities. Don't forget that. Your dad's passing made you head of the household, Tom. We're reliant on you now."

He gazed at her, confused, not really taking in the meaning of her words. The outline of her head and body, dark against the bright window, stirred vague recollections of another place. Other shapes that haunted him still.

"I . . . I thought I was the climber," he muttered, half to himself. "But really . . ."

"*Was* the climber?" his mother cut in once again, and the worry lines deepened about her mouth. "That could be truer than you think. If you don't get a move on, your climbing days may well lie in the past. Then where will we be?"

"Up at the mill, up at the mill," Denny chanted with another grin.

"That's enough cheek from you," his mother said firmly, and she stalked out of the room, dragging Denny with her.

Still slumped on the bed, Tom glanced guiltily at the clock on the shelf. Half past seven! How had he slept so late? And why, after sleeping in, did he feel so tired and heavy? As though he had barely slept at all. Right at that moment he could think of nothing better than sliding back under the blankets and closing his eyes. It wasn't only his mother's inevitable disapproval that stopped him. There was also Jack Steele to be contended with, and the thought of what he might say (and do!) when Tom arrived late. Jack, the foreman of the climbers, whose authority was supreme along the cliffs.

That prospect brought him fully awake, and he hurriedly pulled on his work clothes. Last of all he eased his feet into his heavy climbing boots – boots that had cost him the whole of his first week's pay. Without bothering to lace them up, he clumped downstairs to the flagstoned kitchen where his mother was waiting with a mug of tea and a bacon sandwich.

"Early or late," she said, her voice softer now, though her face retained its lined, anxious quality, "I won't have you going off on an empty stomach. Not to that kind of work especially. Here, get this into you."

He gulped down the tea and bit hungrily into the bread. His lunch sack was standing ready on the table and, still chewing his breakfast, he slipped the strap over his shoulder and made for the door.

"If you've had a change of heart, lad," his mother said quietly, "now's the time to speak."

He stopped and turned to face her. "Change?"

"You know I never wanted you to go for a climber. I

only agreed because you seemed so set on it. And because of what your dad said, about there being no real life without danger. That's something he understood as much as anyone."

The mention of his father, never easy for Tom to deal with, made him reach hastily for the door handle.

"I'm late, Ma," he replied impatiently. "What are you getting at?"

She hesitated. "Only . . . only that there's no shame in admitting that the climbing's too much for you. Never mind what others may say. It's your life to do with as you please. So if you want to alter course – to accept Mr Crawford's offer of the office work – you know I'll back you. I'd even agree to the mill if that's what you decided."

"Up at the mill, up at the mill," Denny broke in, resuming his chant.

"Hush!" she said, and pulled his young body against hers. Then to Tom: "I don't like to see you skulking in bed, that's all. If you're really scared, it's better to give up the work. All I ask is that you don't turn fisherman. After what happened to your Dad I couldn't bear . . ."

But nor could Tom – the thought of his father's death bringing with it the ache of grief – and quickly he leaned forward and kissed his mother on the mouth, silencing her.

"It's okay, Ma," he said. "All I did was oversleep. Honest. I'm not interested in Mr Crawford's offer. You know me, I'd die of boredom in the town clerk's office. Climbing's still the only thing I want."

Which was true. Like every young person for miles around, he had dreamed of spending his adult life as a climber. It was partly the danger of the job that attracted him. And partly the romance. For as long as he could remember, the idea of scaling the high cliffs had conveyed a nobility of purpose, a sense of striving, that no other occupation offered. To fall from the cliffs was somehow tragic; to survive them was a triumph of the spirit. Rightly or wrongly, foolishly or otherwise, that was how the task of climber had always been viewed, not just by Tom, but by all the generations that had gone before.

"Yes, it's the only thing I want," he repeated forcefully, and kissed his mother for the second time, to reassure her.

"Ah, I can see the romance of it is in your bones," she conceded with a sigh, and let him go – out into a day that was neither wholly winter nor spring. The wind gusty and sharp, with a welcome freshness about it.

Late as he was, he lingered on the step for some moments, finishing his sandwich and taking in the familiar scene. The entire town lay spread out before him. Over to his right loomed the blackened pit-heads of the mine. On the opposite ridge stood the mill, a gloomy collection of dull grey buildings, their narrow windows like unsightly gashes in the brickwork. The valley between was filled with row upon row of poor workers' cottages, all identical to the one he had just left, their slate roofs hazy with smoke from the nearby railway yards. Further down the valley, not only the cottages, but the land itself stopped abruptly, the town's industrial grime giving way to the clear purity of the sea. Between land and water, dividing them sharply, there rose the hard line of the cliffs – a line interrupted only once, where the forbidding, craggy shape of Tower Rock thrust like a dark finger into the blue.

The sight of the cliffs, as always, drew him irresistibly, and he clattered off along the street, glancing curiously at the shiny new automobiles that had recently made an appearance in the town.

At that time of morning the streets were mainly deserted, and he was half-way down the hill before he glimpsed someone he knew. A thin, oddly twisted figure, dark-eyed and watchful, who stood huddled in a shallow doorway.

Her name was Deirdre, though amongst the climbers she was known as Blossom, because like a blossom she had fallen early. From the Spire some said. From Tower Rock, said others. Either way, she was lucky to be alive. Or was she? Her body now too crippled by the fall for her ever to climb again; the great adventure of life on the cliffs over almost before it had begun.

She nodded distantly to him as he drew level. He waved back, so filled with pity for her that he was already well past before a disquieting suspicion darted into his mind. Could she possibly have been his dark-eyed companion in that . . . that . . . Where had it been? The sketchy image of a bleak, frozen place rose before him. Fleetingly, he felt again a mittened hand clutching onto his; a frail body fluttering bird-like against his side as they had hung together from an icy cliff. Then, down in the railway yards, an engine shrieked, scattering his thoughts. He whirled around, but Blossom, like those incomplete images, was gone. Even when he tried to picture her as she was in real life – as she had appeared to him moments earlier, there in the windblown street – he could recall only the way she had been before her fall: a pretty girl with a slim graceful body and a face full of laughter.

Feeling only vaguely disturbed by his brief encounter, he ran on, too conscious of his lateness to look back, and therefore unaware of her dark figure shadowing him from street to street.

The jagged lip of the cliffs was close now. Close enough for him to see occasional flashes of brilliant blue-and-white tossed skywards by the wind: the first of the "nesters", migratory birds that usually arrived in the early weeks of spring. Yet here already! With the winter hardly over and the cliffs not yet prepared for their arrival. Every possible climber would be needed, even the old and retired, and he, Tom, had chosen this of all mornings to sleep late!

Cursing his bad luck, he raced past the last line of houses and plunged down the zig-zag stairway that led to the tiny harbour nestling at the base of the cliff. As he leaped from one level to the next, he allowed himself for the second time that morning to think of Jack Steele. How had his mother put it? "If you're really scared . . ." She had been referring to his work as a climber, whereas in fact it was only Jack whom he

12

feared. Jack, with his rock-hard body and mind to match.

He was waiting for Tom on the shingle beach beside the harbour. Behind him the cliff rose vertically for well over a hundred metres, like a craggy extension of his broad shoulders and wiry black hair. As his name suggested, there was no give in him. His eyes, a cold metal-blue, seemed to slice into Tom as they moved from his dishevelled hair down to his untied boots.

"So you're quitting on me already, are you, boy?" he sneered. "All talent and no nerve, is that how it is with you?"

Tom knew better than to make excuses. "I have the nerve," he answered levelly.

Jack ignored his reply. "Or are you one of this new breed who believes in better times long past? The good old days when we were as free as the birds themselves?"

"Better times?" Tom did not understand.

"Every generation or so there's a new crop of them," Jack went on. "A small band of troublemakers who think they can turn the clock back and bring in the golden age of yesteryear. People like Crawford, with his crazy talk and his crazy ideas." He gave a harsh laugh and jerked his thumb towards the heights. "Well, Tower Rock soon sorts them out. It shows them up for what they are: hopeless dreamers who lack the stomach for the real world."

He paused and shot Tom a sharp questioning glance. "Are you a dreamer, Tom Roland?"

The question caught Tom off guard, reminding him suddenly of an icy, barren place where . . . where what? "I . . . I don't know what you're talking about," he stammered.

But again Jack wasn't listening. He had dropped his gaze and was scuffing the shingle with his booted toe, the movement keeping time with the low swish of the surf.

"Well, maybe you are and maybe you're not," he muttered moodily. "Whatever the truth of it, the time's come to put you to the test."

He swung around, his arm raised, and for one terrible moment Tom thought he would point to Tower Rock, which no one had ever climbed, not even Jack. Then, thankfully, his hand moved on and he pointed instead to the Spire – a needle-shaped splinter of cliff that had detached itself from the rest of the coastline, its base half-ringed by exploding surf.

"There!" Jack said, stabbing his finger at the spindle-thin summit. "Up near the top where the birds are mobbing. That's where I want you working today."

"But I'm only an apprentice!" Tom protested. "You said yourself I wouldn't work the heights until . . ."

"That was before you gave me reason to doubt you," Jack broke in. "Now I need to know what you're made of. So get to it." And he strode off across the shingle.

Left to himself, Tom resisted the desire to look again at the Spire. That would only have made matters worse. Outwardly calm, but with a tight knot in the pit of his stomach, he collected a heavy back-pack from a barge in the harbour; and minutes later, in a welter of spray and bird-cries, he was scrambling across the causeway at the opposite end of the beach.

He felt better once he was above the level of the waves. Gradually, as his body accustomed itself to the act of climbing, so the knot in his stomach began to loosen. He was reassured also by the presence of other climbers: silent men who nodded to him in greeting. He passed the last of them about half-way up, and after that he was alone, the wind gaining in power as he mounted higher.

Here, on the upper portion of the Spire there were no obvious hazards. No glass-smooth walls of rock or outward-leaning slopes. The whole surface, scoured by the salt-laden wind, had been eroded into a lacework of crannies and crevices that offered any number of hand- and footholds. Yet it was this very surface, apparently so safe, which put the climber's life at risk. For the rock, eroded to the limits of its natural strength, was forever liable to crumble beneath the weight of a booted foot.

Climbing with extreme caution now, Tom tested

every hold, stamped first on every ledge before bearing downwards. "Think through every move before you make it," he told himself repeatedly. But with the newly-arrived birds wheeling about his head, jostling for the best nesting places, it was difficult to concentrate. Their shrill cries, louder than the wind, their flapping wings, were all too distracting. They became even more frantic and demanding once he began distributing the nesting materials. As he reached into his pack for the small bundles of sticks and cotton waste, they crowded in upon him, their wings buffeting his ears.

"Keep away!" he cried, and swept outwards with his free hand.

Abruptly the whole Spire seemed to shift sideways. The sky tilted above him. For an instant he lost all sense of where he was. Overcome by panic, he imagined himself in another place: in a dead and frozen landscape; the sky on the point of tearing loose from the horizon; the whole world about to be punctured by light.

It was Jack's voice, harsh and pitiless from the nearby cliff, that recalled him to the present. "Get on with it, boy! There isn't time for your foolery!"

He looked down, to where shards of rock were spinning away beneath his feet, and realised that it wasn't the Spire that had swung sideways, but himself. His foothold had collapsed and he was hanging by one hand, the wind snatching at his body. He reached up, but again the rock gave way. Now he was sliding downwards! Slowly at first, then gathering speed, his legs rigid with terror, his fingers clutching desperately at the crumbling surface.

With a jolt his feet struck a ledge which sagged ominously and held. The panic was back, however, his hands feeble and useless, his body cold with sweat. All he could think of was the girl called Blossom. This was how she must have fallen, slipping and sliding helplessly until that moment when her body arced into space and plummeted to where the spray-soaked reef . . . !

He shivered and looked down once again, which was

something he had been taught never to do. The reef was hidden from view – he was glad of that – the sea reduced to a frosted mirror beneath him. Near at hand lay the harbour, a perfect miniature of itself, with tiny boats sitting idle along the quay. In a boat identical to one of those, his father had sailed off for the last time. Only the unbearably painful memory of his face and voice remained. A voice that spoke to Tom now, through the deafening shriek of wind and terror.

"When death finally steps up to greet you, do the right thing and shake him by the hand," he had said and laughed. "In the meantime, death's not a companion to give much thought to."

. . . not a companion to give much thought to.

As the truth of those words struck home, all Tom's panic left him.

"I want you down from there!" Jack was roaring out. "Down, d'you hear?"

For once Jack's orders did not seem to matter. Slowly and deliberately, his ear attuned to the softer, kinder voice that had guided him through childhood, Tom resumed his climb. Up past where he had been before; up towards the spindly summit, a needle of rock so thin that it seemed to sway in the wind. When he could venture no higher, he rested awhile, his eyes fixed longingly on the empty horizon from which his father had never returned. That his father was gone forever was one of those harsh facts which the irrational side of Tom still refused to accept; which he *could not* accept, try as he might. The loss was like a wound in his mind that had failed to heal. The best he could ever do was to bind it in forgetfulness.

He did that now, by giving himself completely to his work. Turning his eyes away from the sea, he began his slow descent – climbing down and round in a spiral motion that enabled him to leave nesting materials in every possible cranny.

The midday break had come and gone by the time he had emptied his pack. On weary legs he descended to the causeway and trudged up to where Jack was again waiting for him on the shingle.

"So now we're playing at heroes, are we?" he jeered. "It's not enough for us to climb the Spire. We have to risk life and limb for all to see."

"You told me I was being tested," Tom answered defensively.

"Aye, so you were. And you've proved what I suspected all along."

"What was that?"

Jack thrust his thumbs into the waistband of his trousers and leaned forward. "I learned years ago that there are two sorts of people in our line of work. Climbers and fallers. Well, after your performance this morning, it's my honest opinion that you're a faller."

"But I didn't fall," Tom protested. "You saw me. I slipped, that was all."

Jack smiled suggestively. "I saw you all right. And d'you know who you reminded me of? The girl they call Blossom. Both of you the same: all talent and no caution. It's a dangerous combination, as she discovered. Too dangerous for this game."

His last words were spoken with such finality that Tom had to struggle to hide his deep disappointment.

"So . . . so you're paying me off?"

"That I'm not," Jack said flatly. "I'm all for pushing you to see how far you'll go. If you ask me, that'll be no great distance. Now take your break," he added, already turning away. "You'll need what strength you can muster for the hours ahead."

With that closing threat, Jack returned to patrolling the cliff, leaving Tom feeling dejected as well as tired.

"Damn you, Jack Steele!" he muttered, and he collected his lunch sack and sank down on the shingle.

Usually, no matter how hard the work, a good midday meal revived him; but on that particular day it merely added to the weariness which had dogged him since first waking. The two hefty cheese-and-onion sandwiches sat like lead in his stomach; and his bottle of cold sweet tea left him all the more drowsy. He leaned back, intending to rest only for a few minutes, and immediately felt himself drifting off – the swish of the surf and the cries of the nesters growing hazy and

17

distant. He made a half-hearted attempt to bring himself back, and failed.

"Why not?" he thought idly, sinking deeper. "Why . . . ?"

But on the very point of succumbing to sleep, he was troubled by a sense of alarm; by the faintest possible whiff of danger. Not the danger of high places. Something else, more profound and disturbing. Vainly he tried to struggle back, but it was too late. With an almost audible click, the gateway to the day had closed behind him.

3 Something closed softly behind him, leaving him in darkness. A narrow opening lay directly in his path. Or rather he thought of it as an opening, though really it was more like a pale rift in the shadows. A crossing point he had used once before.

Before?

Then, there had been silent voices urging him on. Now there was only silence. Less than silence. Nothing. A strange emptiness, an absence, that warned him to venture no further. But why? What reason could there be for holding back? And driven on by curiosity, he ducked down and through . . . out onto the sheer side of the petrified valley.

The valley itself was sunk in night, a bottomless black abyss that opened abruptly at his feet. The only light came from the ice-bound cliff which gave off a pale green glow just bright enough for him to see that he was on the far side of the valley, crouched outside the heavy timber door. It stood ajar, but not invitingly. The broken icicles all along the lintel had taken on the likeness of shattered teeth in a gaping mouth. Teeth that challenged him to keep his distance.

He leaned forward, hesitantly, and peered around the door. The interior of the room, lit by the same unearthly glow as the ledge on which he crouched, looked as dim and cheerless as when he had first come upon it. No ring of welcoming faces awaited him now. No warmth. No flickering firelight. The hearth lay blackened and cold; the walls and ceiling were completely iced over.

And what of the old man? Like the cold and drab interior, had he also returned, his ancient body more stark and wasted than the valley?

19

Tom pushed at the door which refused to budge, its hinges frozen solid, as though denying him entry. He leaned his shoulder against it, intending to force it open enough for him to see the bed along the side wall. Still it resisted, possessed of a will of its own, or so it seemed. Impatient now, he shoved even harder, and with a crack the hinges gave way, his momentum pitching him inside.

The extreme cold struck at him like an invisible weapon. Hunched over defensively, he needed some moments to catch his breath and blink the tears from his eyes.

Through ice-fringed lashes he inspected his poorly lit surroundings. The low bed was still there, its clawed feet frozen to the floor, and its plank base still loosely covered with the sheepskin rug. There was no sign of the old man.

Cautiously, he crept nearer and twitched a corner of the rug aside, sure that all life had fled the valley . . . only to find himself staring down at the tiny body of the child, warm and alive in spite of its stark setting. Left untended, it slept on, its eyelids quivering in response to untold dreams.

He stared down at it, wondering at the elfin delicacy of its features – the thin bow of its mouth, the slightly upturned nose, the golden aureole of hair. It was a face that hovered on the edge of beauty; a face that somehow hid its true character behind closed eyes. Awake, alert, it could have told him anything. Asleep, almost beautiful, it merely hinted at the person within, tempting him to guess at what he would one day find there.

He gave in to the temptation and imagined gentle eyes, soft and grey. Eyes like those of someone he had lost; of someone very dear to him, who had been snatched cruelly away. Yes! he thought excitedly (yearningly?), already convinced that he had discovered the child's secret self, and was rewarded by a smile of recognition which flickered over the sleeping face. Further encouraged, he was reaching down when a cry sounded through the night.

It was not the silent bird-like cry made by the companions. Piercing and more strident, it sent him scurrying outside to inspect the valley. Beyond the ledge, all was darkness as before, and he could see nothing. He waited, and the cry rang out again. Other voices soon answered, distant yet threatening, and he stiffened and backed off. For he had guessed what they were after. Not him so much as the child. Like dogs on a scent, they were hunting it down.

He rushed back to the bed and began wrapping the child in the rug, determined to save it. Before he had finished, there was another, less threatening cry. A warning note, husky and uncertain, carried to him on the wind. It was echoed by others of its kind, all of them drawing him back. Presences that seemed to pluck at his arms, his clothes, and wrench him upwards.

He was half ready for what came next – for the way the entire room heaved and swayed, as if shaken by a giant hand. The noise increased as countless bird-cries broke in upon him; and unable to resist any longer, he rose to meet them.

4 Someone was bending over him. He could see the
outline of a head ringed with countless bird
shapes, their raucous cries almost drowning out
the one persistent voice.

". . . sleep . . . never alone . . . !"

Dazzled by sunlight, he sat up on the shingle.

". . . never alone . . . !"

The words, oddly hoarse and strangled, could have
come from only one person – her neck and throat,
damaged by the fall, making it difficult for her to speak.

"Blossom!" he said aloud.

She flinched, and he wished instantly that he could
have taken the name back.

"I . . . I meant Deirdre," he stammered.

She shook her head, dismissing the question of her
name, intent on something else entirely. "You . . . climber
now . . . must never sleep alone . . . by day . . . never!"

The effort of speech left her strained and breathless,
her closing words so faint that he had to lean forward
to catch them.

"Never?" he pressed her. "Why not?"

But already she was casting nervous glances along
the beach. There was a lull in the even swish of the
surf, and at the sound of approaching footsteps she
fixed him once more with her dark eyes, by way of a
final warning, and then ran for the cover of the nearby
harbour.

Moments later Jack Steele appeared around a curve
in the cliff. He was hurrying, which was unusual, his
face flushed with suppressed excitement.

"You!" he cried as soon as his eyes lighted on Tom. "What are you still doing here?"

Tom stood up, too surprised to do more than stare back at him.

"Don't act the innocent with me, boy," Jack said accusingly. "You were asleep. Isn't that about it? Catching a bit of shut-eye while others are doing an honest day's work."

Normally Tom would have owned up, but being accused like that brought out all his stubbornness. "I was resting, that's all," he lied. "Taking my break, the way you said."

"Taking your break's one thing," Jack replied. "Sleeping's another thing entirely."

"I slept more than my fill last night. You know that. It's why I was late."

Jack eyed him suspiciously, clearly unconvinced. "Then what are you doing here, young Roland? You should be back on the Spire, finishing the job you started. And while you're at it . . ." He paused, momentarily undecided, and then took a long breath, like someone who has just reached a momentous decision. ". . . while you're at it make the most of your good fortune, because I'm warning you now, come Monday it's Tower Rock for you." He nodded vigorously, as if to confirm the rightness of his own judgment. "What's more I'll brook no argument on the matter, so you can save your breath. It's Tower Rock or nothing. That'll tell us how awake you are."

Never in his whole life had Tom felt more wakeful than he did at that instant. Or more shaken. Tower Rock! The name alone was enough to cast a shadow upon the day. As for the thing itself! The mere thought of having to climb it left him pale and speechless, too shocked even to protest as Jack stalked off.

Yet stunned as he was, he understood that it would be a waste of time complaining about the unfairness of it all. To Jack or anyone else come to that. As foreman, Jack was a law unto himself along the cliffs; and as everyone knew, he wasn't a man to change his mind. Nor was he given to speaking lightly. No, if Jack said

23

that he, Tom, must climb the Rock, then unreasonable or not, that was his appointed task, from which there could be no drawing back.

Standing there on the deserted beach, Tom was taken by a brief fit of shivering. Reluctantly he raised his eyes to the heights. Tower Rock had never looked quite so daunting: a great brooding structure, topped by a head-shaped eyeless mask, that dominated land and sea alike. So much taller than the rest of the cliffs that some said it wasn't a natural formation at all, but the remains of an ancient fortress eroded long ago by the encroaching sea. Others again claimed that it was haunted, and they told stories of a legendary climber who, having reached the top, had been marooned there. Whatever the truth, few climbers had ever challenged it; and over the years, those who had been foolish or daring enough to try had ended up either dead or crippled on the reef below.

Was that to be his destiny? Tom asked himself, careless of the incoming tide that lapped at his heels. To end his life on the spray-soaked reef? And why? It made no sense that he could see. None at all. What had he ever done to Jack to deserve such a fate? What lay behind Jack's desire to test him? To *destroy* him? For that was surely his purpose.

The shivering took Tom again, and continued to do so throughout the remainder of the afternoon. Regardless of how hard he worked or how desperately he climbed, still his fear and his bewilderment stalked him. Clinging to a crumbling ledge, he would hear again Jack's words – ". . . come Monday it's Tower Rock for you" – and the dangers of the Spire forgotten, he would turn, squinting in the sunlight, and gaze with dread at the Rock's wind-polished sides and perilous overhangs.

Jack's piercing whistle, which signalled the end of the day's work, came as no relief. It merely brought Monday that much closer. In a mood that matched the gloom of the deepening twilight, he trudged up the stairs to the top of the cliff. Blossom crept silently in his wake, keeping him always in view, but for the present she seemed of little importance.

At that time of evening, and on the last day of the working week, the town was astir with life and energy. In all the major thoroughfares there were rows of stalls and barrows selling everything from food and clothing to nick-nacks and cheap jewellery. Song and laughter spilled from the corner pubs. Shoppers milled about, their faces aglow in the electric lights that had recently replaced the old gas lamps. So much carefree activity, and none of it of any concern to him. He felt almost irritated by it. All he wanted was to reach home and lock himself away, to be alone with his fear.

These dismal thoughts were suddenly interrupted by a burly figure who blundered across the road and shouldered him aside.

"Watch out . . . !" Tom began, and stopped as he recognised the beefy fresh-cheeked face staring down at him.

It belonged to Casey Mallick, a boy he had fought with all through his childhood. Strangely, none of that old enmity now showed on Casey's face.

"Tom!" he burst out, and caught him up in a bear-hug that forced the air from Tom's lungs. "By God, it's good to see you! How long has it been? Six months? A year?"

It did not feel that long to Tom. He seemed to recall a much more recent meeting, whose memory made him shiver, from cold rather than dread. Though when he tried to pin the memory down, to give it a time and place, it slipped beyond reach and vanished.

"Yes . . ." he replied vaguely. "It's been a while."

An arm fell warmly across his shoulders as he moved off up the street, and Casey lurched along beside him.

"Your leg," Tom said, surprised at how badly he was limping. "What happened?"

"Oh that," Casey answered carelessly, and punched at his thigh. "An accident up at the mill. They said I was lucky not to lose the leg altogether. I might have done but for Mr Crawford. 'Casey's strong,' he told them. 'Leave him be and he'll pull through.' Because he's the Town Clerk, they listened, and as usual he was right. The leg . . . well, it works more or less. That's something to be grateful for."

"Yes, something," Tom agreed, not knowing what else to say.

"Anyway, that's enough about my woes," Casey went on, as cheery as ever. "What about you? How have you . . . ?" He stopped, suddenly serious. "What a fool I am!" he said impatiently. "There was that business with your dad, wasn't there? I'm sorry about that, Tom. He was a good man. Too good for this sad old town, or for dark days like these. His boat went down with all hands, I believe."

Tom nodded, not trusting himself to speak, the memory of that fateful day still cruelly fresh in his mind.

"I hear you took it badly," Casey added. "And why not? What's a small injury like mine compared with the loss of a father? Loss, now there's an injury of sorts, one I'd rather not suffer from. And you and your dad so close and all. It must have been like losing your right hand I shouldn't wonder. The kind of handicap you'll carry with you for a while yet. Some, they claim, never get over that sort of thing."

His arm tightened warmly around Tom's shoulder, and he too grew silent, in sympathy with Tom's unspoken grief.

"Mind you," he continued at last, some of his former cheeriness returning, "it's not all bad news. I also hear you're the best young climber we've had in years. There are those who are saying you'll be the one to conquer Tower Rock."

Tom winced at the idea. "They must have been talking to Jack Steele," he muttered resentfully.

"Jack Steele!" Casey's grip tightened even further. "You don't have to worry about him. He's a has-been compared with you. I was only saying as much to Mr Crawford the other day."

It was the second time that name had been mentioned within a space of minutes. As if summoned by it, Mr Crawford's thin, stooping form emerged from a nearby alley and fell into step beside them.

"Good evening to you," he said, and gave Tom an ingratiating smile, peering at him through gold-rimmed spectacles. "Do you mind if we walk together for a while?"

Tom was too taken aback to object, while over to his left the limping figure of Casey melted away into the darkness.

"A fine boy, that one," Mr Crawford commented. "Totally dependable. I'd trust him with my life. So could you, Tom, believe me."

Again Tom said nothing, wondering at the purpose of this obviously prearranged meeting.

They had by then left the noise and bustle of the town behind. The street ahead, lined on either side by poor terraced housing, and dark except for regular pools of lamplight, was completely empty, its silence broken only by their footfalls.

"Ah yes," Mr Crawford continued. "Young Casey has seen the error of his ways. It's the accident did it to him, as you might well appreciate. It gave him new eyes, so to speak. He realises now how important you are to us."

Tom thought at last he understood what was happening: he was being offered an escape route, an alternative to Monday's climb. Compared with the spectre of Tower Rock, it was too tempting to refuse.

"If you're talking about the job you offered me in the Council offices," he said quickly, "then I've changed my mind. I'd like to take it."

He was met by a whinny of high laughter that echoed along the deserted street. "Council offices indeed!" Mr Crawford slipped a pale finger beneath his glasses to wipe the tears from his eyes. "There's no job for you there, Tom. Not any more. You're destined for greater things than office work. We all know that."

"We?"

"Why, those of us who believe there's something better than this." And he raised his hand and indicated the light-studded darkness of the town.

"Better?" Tom asked in a guarded voice, recalling Jack Steele's words to him that morning. "In what way?"

Mr Crawford stopped in mid-stride, his thin shoulders

hunched against the misty cold blowing in from the sea. "In every way, Tom," he answered with sudden passion. "Just think of it. A world where boys like Casey don't have their legs mangled in the vile machinery of the mill. Or . . . or . . ." He clicked his fingers, and as if by magic a shadowy form, unnoticed until then, slipped past them and into a neighbouring doorway. " . . . or where girls like Blossom don't fall from impossible heights." He pointed next to the dark space of the sea, his voice taking on an unexpected note of intimacy. "Or where a boy's beloved father need not risk his life in the wrack and ruin of the storm in order to feed his family. That's something for *you* to consider, Tom."

There was a loud clatter as Tom stepped hastily backwards, his booted feet slithering on the cobblestones.

"Yes, that's the world we believe in," Mr Crawford added in the same passionate tone, pointing now at him. "And so do you in your heart. You who can no more give up your beloved father than you can those wonderful climbing skills you've been blessed with."

"But my father's dead," he protested, having to wrench the truth out of himself. "Casey and Blossom are both crippled. Nothing can change any of that. It all happened in the past."

Mr Crawford's glasses caught and held the misty lamplight, two pallid moons staring intently at him. "Do you believe the past is dead and gone, boy? That we can't make it live again? Restore the lost and lame to what they were? I tell you that's not so." He leaned forward, suddenly secretive. "Consider this: a fragment of the past still exists, right here amongst us. Enough to make a difference. It's waiting for us to give it life, breath. Once that's done, everything will change. All that this town has become, all its mines and machines and misery, will be wiped away. Replaced by better times. By other, older, wiser ways."

The two pallid moons blinked out as Mr Crawford shuffled a step nearer. In the yellowish lamplight his face was gaunt and strained.

"Well?" he insisted in a tense whisper. "What do you say?"

Tom gazed warily up and down the street, feeling peculiarly unnerved by the ardour of this man whom he had always thought of as sober and settled.

"You're not the only one who's talking about these things," he said. "Jack Steele's also having his say. He reckons that people who want to turn the clock back are troublemakers and dreamers."

"Dreamers?" The high laughter rang out once again. "Well, for once Jack Steele is near the mark. Yes, dreamers, true enough, as you and I know full well. What a dream it is, though, Tom. To seek out the Sleeper himself. To wake him from . . ."

He broke off, his head cocked towards the sound of approaching voices.

"The Sleeper?" Tom queried sharply.

But as with Casey before him, Mr Crawford had melted away into the night.

Within minutes a group of miners came labouring up the hill, their eyes like pale circles in the blackened masks of their faces.

"What's this we hear, young Tom?" they called out. "Are you set to test yourself against Tower Rock now?"

"If you fall, you'd do well to make a good job of it," one of them added cheerfully. "The name Blossom won't sit easily on a young chap like yourself."

Still laughing at the joke, they trooped off down a side street, leaving Tom to complete the rest of his journey alone.

If he had expected to find sanctuary at home, he was mistaken. His mother was waiting in the tiny living room, her face almost as grey from worry as the wisps of hair that fell about her cheeks.

"Is it true what they're saying about you and the Rock?" she challenged him.

He nodded, dropping wearily into the nearest chair.

"What in God's name got into you, boy?" she burst out angrily. "Do you think you're so much better than all the others who've tried and failed?"

"It's not my idea, Ma. It was Jack's ruling."

"Then I'll talk to him. I'll tell him to his face how the cliffs are just lumps of stone and nought else, and how there's nothing noble about scaling them, never mind what folk say. While I'm alive, I'll not let him make a hero of you. Nor a martyr neither."

"It won't do any good," Tom pointed out. "You know what he's like."

Denny, in awe of his brother for the first time in his young life, crept forward to touch his hand. "Can you do it, Tom? Can you get to the very top?"

"He'll never find out," his mother answered for him. And to Tom: "I won't let it happen. I'm telling you that right now. We've lost one man in this family already. That's enough. It's all the payment I'll ever make to this town. And I'll not be swayed by all the talk of legendary climbers and how honoured I should be to number you amongst them. A dead hero is dead still, that's what I say."

To mark the end of the discussion, she marched out to the kitchen and brought in his dinner. "Here," she said. "Maybe a full belly will help put some sense into your head."

After a hard day's work he was usually hungry, but not today. He took only a few mouthfuls, pushed the plate aside, and walked over to the door.

"I'm too old to hide behind your apron, Ma," he told her gently. "If I did, I'd be a laughing stock."

Her voice, tearful and desperate, followed him up the stairs. "Better a laughing stock than a broken body on the shore."

Lying alone in his room, he tried to sleep, to leave behind in the waking world all the anxiety that had dogged him through the day, but even that was denied him. Hours passed, and still he was staring at the ceiling, the pattern of cracks in the old plaster reminding him more and more of a cliff-face as the night wore on. Shortly before dawn he was close to giving up, ready to go downstairs and make himself a pot of tea. What stopped him were the first faint hints of birdsong, the awakening birds calling feebly through the darkness. Tired out by his long vigil, he imagined for a moment that they were singing for him. He closed his eyes, to hear them more clearly, and immediately they were transformed into human voices. Eager, shrill with impatience, they beckoned for him to follow them out into the night. Before he could resist, he was asleep.

5 They were waiting for him in the firelit room, as they had before, a half circle of eager faces. The only visible signs of his lateness were the depleted store of wood beside the fire and the hint of impatience in their watchful eyes. In obedience to their unspoken wishes, he held out his arms, and Casey (for it was him, despite the Puck-like quality of his features) handed Tom the warmly wrapped child. Simultaneously, Blossom (yes, her too) mouthed words he had heard once before and since forgotten.

"You are the Carrier."

"The Carrier?" he queried aloud, his voice as hollow as the room itself.

They nodded, smiling their support and encouragement, and there, in that particular place, it was somehow answer enough. Yes, he was the Carrier. He even half understood when Blossom took the child from him and placed it carefully in the now empty pack on his back. Through his sheepskin jacket he could feel its warmth seeping into him; the enormous vitality, stored in its tiny body, added to his own strength and readiness.

At a signal from Casey, he moved towards the door and listened. As he had expected, there were sounds of pursuit coming from outside – a group of hunters drawing ever nearer – and quickly he led his companions out into the bitter cold of a waning day.

How late it was already. The sky, blank and starless, was darkening above them, the valley growing hazy and uncertain as the shadows deepened. An icy wind had risen, lifting the powdery snow from the top of the opposite cliff and driving it into their faces. Above the line of that same cliff a speck of

32

black appeared. It rose higher, resolved itself into the outline of a man, and straight away a loud hallooing broke out.

Tom had no need of Blossom's soft whimpering to urge him on. Turning on the narrow ledge, he faced the cliff which soared above him, its frozen surface polished to a mirror smoothness by the wind. He could not possibly have climbed it unaided, but with his own ice-axe in one hand and Casey's in the other, he was able to claw his way up, the uncoiled rope trailing below.

There was an overhanging lip near the top, and he paused before tackling it, to gather his strength. That was when he saw the face: the ghostly likeness of himself that stared out from the polished surface. It was his own face, there was no doubt about that. Yet as with the child – as with Blossom and all the others – the features were subtly changed, touched by a vaguely elfin quality. His chin appeared a little too pointed, his nose a little too upturned, his eyes narrowed by raised cheekbones. And his ears . . . !

He struck hastily at the polished surface, and the unnatural image disappeared behind a maze of cracks. Then, hand-over-hand, his body dangling in space, he hauled himself around the overhang to safety.

Tiredness alone did not cause him to lie panting in the powdery snow at the top; nor was it just the cold that made his teeth chatter. That face! Those ears! Those dark slits for eyes! What had he become? Or had he merely glimpsed a distortion in the ice? A warped mirror image? But then why were Blossom and the others also changed? All of them drawn towards a common likeness?

He was recalled to the task at hand by a sharp tug on the rope. It alerted him to the appearance of several black-clothed figures on the opposing heights. Before he could be spotted, he stooped below the projecting lip of the cliff. There, safely hidden, he drove both axes deep into the ice and used them to brace himself against the sudden tautness in the rope.

Pursued by hallooing voices, his companions swarmed up towards him. Once again Blossom came last. As she crawled across the lip and sank down exhausted in the snow, the child on his back let out a sigh. Not of complaint. Rather it was the kind of sound made by someone settling contentedly to sleep. None the less it had the same effect on Blossom as a command. Her face still ashen from the effort she had just made, she rose shakily and peered out over the edge. What she saw there clearly alarmed her because she whirled around and pointed to one of her companions: a boy whom Tom recognised, but could not immediately put a name to.

The boy did not protest at being singled out, though his strangely slanted eyes quivered slightly from shock. That one small display of emotion over, he prepared for action. His mittens he tossed aside as if he had no further use for them. He also tore off his cap and muffler, fully exposing his face – a face which made Tom start in surprise, for it was blemished by a livid birthmark that ran from one ear round to the corner of his mouth. Finally he slipped free of his back-pack from which he drew a short-handled cudgel.

Blossom's only reaction to these preparations was to give a curt nod of approval. Casey, on the other hand, embraced the boy warmly, as did the rest of the companions, some of them almost tearful at this leave-taking. Then, with the voices from the valley growing ever louder, they moved off in a tight group, gesturing for Tom to follow.

"You can't leave him here," Tom objected. "Not on his own."

There was a squirming motion in his pack, accompanied by another sigh, and Blossom rushed at him, her eyes smouldering with resentment.

"Carrier!" That word again, mouthed furiously, her mittened hand stabbing at his chest. "Carrier!"

It was like an argument that he had no answer for; but so too was the boy standing guard alone at the head of the cliff. Caught between the two, Tom lingered on, while the child moved restlessly against his back.

The boy, not Blossom, was the one who helped make up his mind. With an encouraging smile, he pushed Tom away, acting as if this lonely guardianship was all that he desired; his face, at that moment, so lit by a sense of hope that the birthmark seemed to fade. And unhappily, feeling oddly shamed by the boy's resolve, Tom traipsed off into the twilight with the others.

They had not gone far when they heard a clash of weapons, followed by a long drawn-out scream, of someone falling from a great height. Tom looked behind him, but the darkness stood like a curtain between him and the cliff-edge; and when

34

he turned questioningly to Blossom, her head was lowered and she gave no sign. What reassured him was the suggestion of relief that rippled amongst the others; the way they increased their pace, with Casey breaking into a lurching run.

They were some distance on before they again heard the sound of conflict. Brief as well as faint, it was over in seconds. Except that this time it ended not with a scream, but in silence. A terrible void that was somehow louder than any cry.

Casey, who was in the lead, stumbled and sank to his knees, his back heaving with emotion. Raising both fists, in anger as well as grief, he brought them crashing down onto the snow. Tom could not see his face, but he had seen Blossom's – how her mouth had twitched once, in bitter recognition, and then set into a hard, unyielding line. Now, her brow furrowed with disapproval, she was dragging at Casey's arm, trying to force him up. When that failed, she punched at him mercilessly, her mittened hands pummelling his head and shoulders until he rose and limped on.

The hallooing had started up again, fainter, but also more insistent than before. A triumphant note had crept into it, as if, despite the darkness, the hunters were feeling sure of their prey. Glancing back, Tom saw at once the reason for their confidence. A broad line of tracks, scored deeply into the snow, stretched away behind. With each footstep, the packed-down snow creaking in protest, he and his companions were marking out a trial. The act of flight itself was betraying them to the hunters.

He was about to call a warning to Blossom when the child again shifted its position. Moving lazily in the confined space of the pack, it made a burrowing motion and nestled close, as though seeking comfort. Or was he, Tom, the one who was being comforted? Was that small, warm body signalling to him that all was well? He faltered, unsure, and immediately a large snowflake brushed softly against his cheek. It was the first of many. Soon countless white flecks were drifting from the blackness of an empty sky. The wind had dropped, so the snow fell straight down through the stillness. Soundlessly, it settled on their lowered heads and hunched shoulders, and also on the tracks left in their wake – blurring the broken edges, filling them, rapidly wiping out all sign of anyone having passed that way.

Muffled by the fast falling snow and the everincreasing distance, the hallooing died away to nothing. All that remained was the eerily silent storm and the crunch and squeal of footsteps on the powdery surface.

Tom tightened the straps of his pack, moved by an impulse to draw the child even closer. "They've lost us!" he called out joyfully, his breath cutting a swathe through the drifting flakes which eddied playfully about his head.

As usual, his companions made no reply, though by now he was able to detect quite clearly those unspoken communications which travelled between them. Wordless, voiceless, like winter birds in flight, their thoughts spiralled and soared in the frosty air, forming intricate patterns against the night.

Satisfied, he moved up beside Casey, matching his limping pace, glad of the others clustered about him. Their combined presence seemed to stand between him and the mysterious perils of this bleak wasteland. They were his guarantee of safety. And of the child's safety too. After all, wasn't he the Carrier? The one chosen, for whatever reason, to dwell at the centre of this warm and caring circle?

He looked around fondly at his companions and noticed how Blossom kept herself aloof from all the rest, her slightly misshapen figure trudging along at the far edge of the circle. Out of the whole group, she alone continued to trouble him. Her dark eyes, so bitter and resentful, filled him with distrust; her face, so coldly attractive, both drew and repelled him.

Sensing that she was being watched, she turned and shot him a look of such hostility that he sucked in his breath and shuddered. It was as if a knife had pierced him, its keen, unfeeling point sliding into the hollow beneath his heart – that secret place he had yet to fill. Even the child felt the shock of it, and huddled down, its tiny hands pressed convulsively into the small of his back. That helped to steady him. As did the way Casey encircled his shoulders with one arm, their two bodies jostling easily together as they walked on.

He was not aware of the snow stopping. He raised his head and the whirling flakes had disappeared, leaving the sky a uniform black once more. Somewhere beyond the blackness lay a world of light – he understood that even then. Light that occasionally peeked past the rim of the horizon or slashed the obscurity overhead with vivid lightning trails. These intrusions

from the outside, each more urgent than the last, might have
bothered him had it not been for his companions. "Not yet,"
they sang in their wordless fashion, their faces frosted as the
old man's had been. As his own surely was. "A little further,
another step, and another." A lilting chant that urged him on.
Their eyes and his, their weirdly elfin features, trained on the
darkness ahead.

It opened to them all at once, like a curtain parting. To
reveal a gleaming forest directly in their path. Trees that
glinted in non-existent starlight. Trees of ice or glass; leaves
as thin and brittle as a curled tongue of hoar-frost. The wind
sighed in welcome when they drew near and threw up glittering sprays of snow that hung like mist beneath the frozen
boughs. On those same boughs were perched the fixed,
transparent shapes of birds, their beady eyes focussed upon
nothing.

The sky flashed and writhed closed, and three of the companions were gone. Those that remained, Tom amongst them,
had entered the forest now. They were walking in the luminous
shadow of leaves that rattled and rang in the wind. "Not yet,"
they chimed, adding to the song. So that Tom forged ahead
even when the sky swallowed more of his companions.

Apart from himself and the child, only Casey and Blossom
remained. They raised their arms together and pointed to a
kind of hillock in the snow, with a low opening at its base. One
after the other they squirmed through, into a cave of sparkling
emptiness, its curving walls festooned with the flash and
gleam of crystal shapes. At the centre of the emptiness lay a
couch of ice. A throne? That was the word which rose in
Tom's mind, and was just as quickly forgotten as Casey was
plucked away by a sudden beam of light.

"There . . ."

Blossom was mouthing the word at him when she was also
struck, though unlike Casey she resisted. Her silent scream
swelled out into the cave, jangling the crystal walls which
boomed and sang in sympathy. Transfixed by light, she
hovered for a while at the very edge of vision, more transparent than the birds in their icy trees. But she could not stay. The
sky thundered again, and her outline slowly faded, vanishing
into the cave's chill air.

The sole survivor, Tom slipped the pack from his shoulders

37

and lifted the baby out. Each moment, he knew, was precious. Not daring to look up, he drew the sheepskin close around the tiny body and placed the living bundle gently on the couch. The child's face, caught in a haze of golden hair, had never appeared more peaceful. Even the blue-veined eyelids had ceased to quiver, as though it had sunk beyond the reach of dreams. Or had it? One shell-like hand groped clear of the coverings and settled on the couch's icy hardness. It did not flinch from the cold.

"See," it seemed to declare. "I am at home here. For me, this is a place of security."

And Tom, ducking his head in mute acceptance, gave himself up to the light.

6 The quality of the light was not what it should have been. Tom rolled over and looked blearily at the clock on the shelf. Its hands were locked together on the twelve. Twelve? His head half-buried in the pillow, he needed a few seconds for the meaning of the number to sink in. Then he was up and out of bed in a single movement.

What day was it? Ah, yes, Sunday. That wasn't quite so serious, but still bad enough.

"Ma?" he called nervously. "Ma?"

There was no answer, which meant that she and Denny had gone to church without him. No, it meant more than that. She must have called and called and finally walked out in a huff.

Hastily, he dressed in his Sunday clothes and pulled a comb roughly through his hair. Was there time to wash? "Cleanliness is next to godliness," his mother was fond of saying. On Sunday, of all days, that carried some weight with him, and he poured water from the jug into the basin and splashed some onto his face. Its cold clinging touch brought with it the unexpected picture of a hand resting on an icy shelf: a surprisingly warm hand despite its resting place, the skin pliant and soft, the nails a shell-like pink. Where had he seen . . . ? But he had no time for such thoughts now, and with his face and hands still wet, he ran downstairs and out into another blustery day.

He was greeted by the sight of Tower Rock: a warning finger set sternly against sea and sky to remind him of what the future held in store. He turned his head away, trying to blot that out too, and slammed the door behind him. Across the road a familiar figure darted into the nearest alleyway, but he was in too much of a hurry to care.

"I know you're there, Blossom," he shouted and ran off, following the line of streets that wound around the hillside – the same hillside that closed off the upper end of the valley.

Below him, on the level space where hill and valley merged, lay the town common. At its edge stood the church, a tall stone building stained almost black by coal-smoke from the mill and the surrounding houses. Originally its steeple had topped Tower Rock, but like the Spire it had been worn away by the salt wind, and all that remained of it now was a discoloured stump.

Tom approached it by taking a short cut across the cemetery. Between gusts of wind he could hear the congregation singing, their voices straining upwards, higher than the shattered remnants of the steeple. The singing stopped, and he eased open the heavy door just as the minister was making his closing comments.

". . . a place in your prayers for the two fine young lads, Alan Makepeace and John Godfrey, who now lie in a coma, deaf to all around them. May they wake from their strange slumber and . . ."

Those two names sent Tom stumbling backwards out of the porch. John Godfrey, only a few years older than himself, he knew as a fellow climber. And Alan Makepeace!

It was similar to when he had splashed cold water onto his skin some ten minutes earlier: a sudden picture flashed before him, this time of a young face disfigured by a livid birthmark. Except that this was not the sort of picture he could easily dismiss. Having gained a name, a positive identity, it was lodged firmly in his mind. Again those puckish lips smiled encouragingly at him; again those oddly slanted eyes, alight with hope, turned slowly but readily towards the darkened space of the valley where . . .

He shook his head in bewilderment and he was back in the blustery spring day. Already people were spilling from the church. Two women, near neighbours of his, stopped beside him, their voices lowered in private conversation.

"There're some who are saying it was the result of a fall," the younger woman murmured. "Personally I have my doubts. Especially where Alan Makepeace is concerned. That mark of his!" She gave a mock shudder to show her distaste. "What does his mother call it? A naevus or some such rubbish. Well, I've often felt like telling her: you'll never hide the truth with outlandish words. Even the doctors can't do that."

Her older companion nodded. "You're right there, Enid. Call it what you like, it's still the Devil's mark. Marge Gower up the road reckons it's a wicked bruise left by the Devil's thumb whenever he claims a child for his own dark purposes."

Tom pushed between them and took the older woman by the shoulders. "What do you know about Alan?" he shouted. "What gives you the right to say such terrible things?"

"Tom!" His mother was dragging at his sleeve. Not to restrain him: only to hug him warmly, her body trembling with emotion. "Thank goodness!" she sobbed, tightening her hold as if she feared he might disappear. "I tried and tried to wake you this morning. And when the minister said . . . when he told us about the young lads in the coma . . . I thought . . . I thought . . ."

Held fast in her arms, all his outrage left him. "There's no need to cry, Ma. Nothing's going to happen to me. I promise."

He had meant only to reassure her, but the moment the words left his lips he realised that he had reached a decision. Come what may, he wasn't going to end up like Alan or Blossom. He would never try and climb Tower Rock, not for Jack or anyone. And with that decision, all the colour and adventure seemed to seep out of his life, to leave the future grey and uneventful. Yet at least there *would* be a future, he consoled himself with that.

"I'm here, Ma," he added softly. "I'm staying."

"If he was mine," the younger woman said, "I wouldn't be hugging him. He'd be feeling the back of my hand."

"Not before time," her companion chimed in.

But he no longer cared what others might think or say. The dark cloud of anxiety, which had hovered over him since the previous afternoon, had suddenly dissolved: Tower Rock had become just another section of cliff; and Monday presented itself as just another working day – one of many that stretched drearily on into a life now devoid of either meaning or romance.

"Come on, Ma," he said, relieved, but also with a bitter taste of defeat on his tongue. "Let's leave them to their gossip." Taking Denny's hand in his, he linked arms with his mother and walked away across the common.

With the church service over, people were standing around on the grass, laughing and talking together. Others had taken off their jackets to play at tag. There were even some who had launched kites into the wind – bright diamonds or rectangles of painted paper which shone like crystals against the overcast sky.

"Look!" Denny crowed, pointing upwards.

Tom followed his direction, but the sight of those crystal shapes prodded uncomfortably at his memory, and he glanced away, to where a group of mill workers had begun a game of football.

One of the players, a burly figure with a limping run, caught his attention at once. Tom raised his hand and was about to call out a greeting when the player turned, and Casey's features scowled dangerously at him. "Who are you staring at, Tom Roland?" he yelled, no friendliness in his voice now. "Go off and

42

join your glamorous climbing mates. There's no room for you here."

"Don't flatter yourself I'm interested in the likes of you," Tom called back, all the old enmity awakening in him. "I'm particular about the company I keep."

"Tell him, Tom," Denny whispered fiercely, his small fists bunching up. "You tell him!"

The next minute, far less certain of himself, he was scampering behind Tom's legs as Casey came at them in a lurching run.

"Hold up, Casey Mallick!" Mrs Roland cried. "You as well, Tom! I won't stand here and watch the pair of you brawling. If you have to fight – and don't ask me why you should – you can do it out of the way of decent folk."

Casey, who had slithered to a halt, was glowering at Tom. "She's right," he said with an unpleasant laugh. "This isn't the time or place for you and me to meet." And to Tom's amazement he closed one eye in a deliberate wink. "There are too many snooping Charlies around here for my liking. What we have to do is best done in secret."

Although he continued to scowl, his knowing wink, plus the message hidden in his closing words, were too obvious for Tom to miss.

"Well, are we agreed about a more secret place?" Casey prompted him, for Tom had said nothing, still too surprised to answer.

". . . er . . . yes . . . another place," he stammered.

"Right, I'll see you there," Casey said, and limped back to his game.

Mrs Roland turned worried eyes on her son, but Tom hardly seemed to notice. He was busy scanning the common, looking for . . . what? Snooping Charlies, Casey had called them. Spies, Tom supposed, out there in the Sunday throng. But why? What could they possibly want with him and Casey? Who could they be? He looked inward, searching his mind for clues, and glimpsed a series of black figures set against a snowy background,

43

their hallooing cries ringing through the waning· day. Were those perhaps the spies? The snooping Charlies? And if so, how did that help him in the here and now? The last of the winter snow had vanished weeks earlier; and nearly everyone on the common was dressed in black, which was normal Sunday attire.

"What's going on, Tom?" his mother asked, her voice tight and anxious.

"I can't say, Ma," he answered truthfully. "It's all a mix-up. Maybe the best thing for us is to get off home."

"Maybe it is," she said, nodding, and with Denny between them they hurried across the common and up the first street they came to.

Even by the standards of the town it was a mean little street, its cobblestones dank and worn, its central gutter slimy with moss, and many of its houses derelict or boarded up. At one point it became particularly narrow, the houses leaning in so far that they obscured half the sky, and it was there that a group of men and woman, led by Jack Steele, stepped abruptly from the surrounding doorways. Still in their dingy work-clothes, they fanned out across the road.

"What do you want with us, Jack?" Mrs Roland challenged him.

He stood astride the gutter, his hands propped on his hips. "Begging your pardon, ma'am," he answered, "but I have no business with you. It's only your son I'm after."

"You'll have to get past me first," she said hotly, and would have moved in front of Tom had he not held her back.

"No, Ma, I can speak for myself," he said, and stepped forward alone. "What is it, Jack? Isn't Monday to Saturday good enough for you? Do you have to act the foreman on a Sunday too?"

"Hush your nonsense, boy," Jack said, his eyes hard and watchful. "There are important things for us to discuss here. Such as the loss of one of my climbers. John Godfrey he was called." As he spoke the name aloud, he watched Tom's face intently, as if looking for some sign. "You wouldn't have heard about him by any chance?"

Tom had to suppress a slight shiver. "I might have," he answered.

There was a shuffle of feet from the people grouped behind Jack, and then a silence disturbed by the hum of wind along the rooftops.

"Don't try and hold out on me," Jack growled. "Just tell me what you know."

Tom blinked nervously, and in that instant of darkness he seemed to hear again a far-off scream. He took a long breath, to steady himself. "They say he's lying in a coma."

"They?"

"The people at the church. Some of them think he must have had a fall."

Jack's eyes were still fixed upon his face, probing past the stiffened muscles of his cheeks.

"And the other one?" Jack asked suspiciously. "Alan Makepeace?"

The shiver was even harder to suppress this second time. "They say he also had a fall."

"A fall? What are you on about, lad? He was a mill worker. There was precious little for him to fall from."

"I'm only telling you what I heard."

Jack sighed and shifted his feet, though he remained as vigilant as ever. "Aah, what a worry you are to me, Tom. That's why I've asked you to tackle the Rock. It's the one sure way of settling the trouble between us."

"How can that settle anything?" Mrs Roland broke in.

"Pride comes before a fall, ma'am. The Rock'll teach him what he can and cannot do. With luck it'll save him from temptation."

"Without luck it'll kill him," she retorted.

"Aye, it could do that too."

"And d'you think I'll keep silent while my own son . . . ?"

Tom pressed a finger gently to her lips. "It's all right, Ma. My mind's made up. I won't be climbing the Rock on Monday. Nor on any other day come to that."

"Even if your job depends on it?" Jack asked.

Although Tom was prepared for exactly that kind of challenge, still the injustice of it took his breath away. "That's not fair!" he burst out.

"Fair or not, it's the only offer you'll get from me."

As ever, he knew there was no point in arguing, not with someone like Jack. But to give up the only job he had ever wished for! Right there in the open street! And at a moment's notice!

"So what's it to be?" Jack pressed him. "Are you ready to do my bidding or do you find some other line of work?"

Tom's mouth had gone completely dry. He glanced round once, quickly, at the Rock looming behind him, and knew he had just one answer to give. "I'll find other work," he said, having to choke the words out.

Jack's muscular body relaxed, as though a heavy weight had been lifted from his shoulders. "You've made the right decision, lad," he said, all the harshness gone from his voice. "The Rock's not for you, despite what others may be whispering. It's not for any mortal man or woman, and don't ever be tempted to think otherwise. Remember the choice you've made today and stick by it. If you don't – and I say this without malice – I'll be forced to hunt you from the heights myself."

"What's all this nonsense?" Mrs Roland cried belligerently. "You order the boy to make the climb, then congratulate him for refusing. Stop talking in riddles and speak plainly to him, man."

Jack gave a casual shrug, though his eyes retained their hard, watchful gleam. "You want plain words? All right then. Your son has too much talent as a climber.

If he'd stayed with me, he'd have grown tired of the ordinary work. Like others before him, he'd have cast his eyes up to the Rock. That's why I had to scare him off. For his own good as much as anyone else's. Before it was too late. There, is that plain enough for you?" And he shouldered Tom aside and clumped off down the street, his followers hurrying after him.

Denny stole out from behind Tom's legs and gazed up into his brother's face. "You're not scared of Jack Steele, are you, Tom? I bet you can climb higher than him if you want to."

"Not any more," Tom answered bitterly. "My climbing days are over. It's the mill for me from here on."

"There's still Mr Crawford's offer," his mother reminded him. "You can take that up."

"No, he won't have me any more," he said, remembering Mr Crawford's oddly worded refusal. "My only choices are the mill or the mine, and I couldn't work underground, not after the climbing."

Denny, sensing the gravity of the situation, failed to break into his usual teasing chant about the mill. "But you've always wanted to climb, Tom," he protested.

"So he has," Mrs Roland agreed grimly, leading the way up the dingy street. "He'd be a climber still but for Jack's envy. For mark my words, that's what lies behind all his riddles. Envy of your talents. The great Jack Steele can't bear the thought of being bested by a boy."

Alone in his room that afternoon, Tom wondered whether his mother was right. Had Jack got rid of him simply out of envy? Or was there more to it than that? Some deeper motive which Jack did not dare reveal? Unless, of course, Jack was somehow involved in that vague jumble of dream images which had come to dog Tom's waking hours. No. He shook his head. That was impossible. Or was it?

To escape his own dark thoughts, he went to the window and looked out into the sunlit day. Although he was too far from the coast to see the birds swooping and diving above the surf, the distant line of the cliffs

47

was enough to rekindle his sense of loss. Because of Jack, never again would he feel the tug of the wind as he stood poised on the cliff-face. Never would he take part in the egg-culling, later in the spring, or any of the other activities – the collection of fine down from the moulting chicks; the gathering of the jewelled flight feathers dropped on the ledges during high summer; the ringing of the young birds in the fading autumn days. And finally, an activity that attracted the wealthiest buyers, the search for the many pearls that littered the nesting sites after the birds' departure. Originally swallowed by the birds on the far side of the ocean, where the flocks fed on oysters in tropic seas, the pearls were the most precious harvest of them all. The reaping of that harvest, in the bright, sharp days of early winter, was the high point of the year for every climber. Though not for Tom. Not any longer. That, like the climbing itself, like the whole annual cycle, was now lost to him forever.

Feeling more betrayed than angry, he stumbled away from the window and flung himself miserably onto the bed. Yet even sleep was denied him, the voice of instinct warning him to remain awake while he could. With nowhere else to turn, he jumped up again and began moving restlessly about his room – pacing up and down for hour after hour, until the day eventually waned into night.

It was quite late when his mother knocked on the door. "Are you awake, Tom?" She sidled in and placed a cup of steaming cocoa on the bedside cupboard. "I understand how disappointed you must feel," she said gently. "The mill's never been what you wanted. Still, at least this way you'll stay alive."

He gave a short unhappy laugh. "I'll stay alive all right, but what for?"

She clicked her tongue in disapproval. "I wonder what your father would have said to that?" she admonished him.

Stricken, as always, by the mention of his father, he

put his arm clumsily around her shoulders. "I'm sorry, Ma. It's just . . ."

"You don't have to explain to me, lad," she said, softening to him. "Now try and get some rest."

She patted his cheek and went over to the door, but on the point of leaving, she hesitated.

"There's one other thing, Tom. Those deep sleeps you've been falling into. Are they tied in with this business of Jack and the Rock?"

He wasn't sure how to answer her. "I expect so . . . I mean . . . it's possible."

"So they'll stop now the climbing's done with?"

Would they? Again he had no ready answer.

"Nobody rests easy in the shadow of the Rock, Ma," he said evasively, but then was struck by the unexpected truth of his own words. "Now the shadow's gone," he went on in a firmer voice, "everything will get back to normal. You'll see."

"I'm glad to hear it, lad," she said, and smiled at him as she closed the door.

Cup in hand, he moved over to the window once again. Was it as simple as all that, he wondered, did it all come down to the Rock and his fear of it? He took a sip of the hot drink, its milky warmth flowing through him. Yes, he thought with sudden resolution: the dreams were probably no more than the product of his own anxiety. As for people like Casey and Blossom and Mr Crawford, they would have given the same attention to anyone who was about to challenge Tower Rock. Blossom especially, after her experience on the cliffs. Well, they could forget about him now. As an ordinary mill worker, he would be of no further interest to them. Like his strange dreams, they would drift out of his life and leave him in peace. Why, they had probably done so already.

Standing there, cup in hand, he was so nearly convinced he was right that the darting movement in the street below caught him by surprise. Pressing his face to the glass pane, he peered down . . . into the pale, upturned face of Blossom. She returned his gaze unflinchingly, her eyes, hollowed out by shadow, instantly shattering all his fragile confidence. She nodded once, briefly, and then, as if to prove to him that nothing had changed between them, she withdrew into the nearest doorway and set herself to wait.

7 She was waiting for him in the crystal chamber, as was Casey. Two protective figures ranged on either side of the frozen couch where the child slept on, its eyelids quivering delicately.

Dreams within dreams, Tom thought, the idea coming to him from another, more distant self. Or were all the dreams one and the same? In which case the child was perhaps the person who . . .

But that was a form of reasoning that had no place in this glittering room, and he let the thought fade into the background. What mattered here was the child, its elusive beauty, the way its elfin mouth twitched into a half-smile of recognition.

Tom moved forward, and Casey, acting as if there were no bad blood between them, clapped him heartily on the shoulder, the weight of his hand feather-light in this rarefied atmosphere.

He received no such welcome from Blossom. Her darkly attractive face glared at him as she lifted the child and placed it in his pack.

"You are the Carrier," she said soundlessly, giving him what he now understood to be the ritual greeting, her full-lipped mouth biting down on the words in a mute act of denial.

He stretched out a hand to thank her, but she slapped it away – another feather-blow that set up icy currents in the stillness of the air. Currents that whirled them towards the low opening and out into a cloud-heavy day.

The remaining companions were already out there, stamping their booted feet on the frozen ground to ward off the cold.

Tom glanced from face to face, searching hopefully for one with a livid birthmark, but there was no sign of Alan, and with a pang of disappointment he realised he was gone forever. Although the others gathered about him, friendly and protective, it was as if a gap had appeared in the circle. An absence that only the close warmth of the child could make up for.

Tom pulled his cap down over his ears and looked around him. In a hollow to his left lay the petrified forest. All its magical quality had fled with the darkness, and now it was no more than a tangle of dull tree-shapes, empty of life or movement. He was glad when Casey made off in the opposite direction, leading the way up over a swell of hillside towards a blank grey horizon.

Tom trudged along in the group, head down, forcing his way through the snow. It was particularly deep here, and whenever possible he trod in Casey's footprints to make the going easier. Beside him, Blossom was finding it hard to keep up. He would have liked to help her, but was wary of another rebuff. Whenever he stole a glance in her direction, her face was creased with pain, her lips strained back against her teeth. Once, she licked at the frost gathered on her lips, and he had to look away, disturbed by the sight. The soft pink of her tongue was like a glimpse of some secret self that stirred feelings in him he would rather have denied.

Several of the others had also begun to stagger with fatigue. How long had they been walking? In this grey, uneventful landscape the passage of the hours meant nothing to him. His only measure of time was the increasing heaviness of the child. As the day became duller, greyer, so the child's weight seemed to grow, until soon the straps of the pack were biting into Tom's shoulders, making it harder and harder for him to plunge on through drifts that sometimes reached up past his thighs.

"Can't we stop?" he gasped.

He had spoken in an ordinary voice, but his words, amplified by the unnatural stillness, boomed out over the snow.

The companions were all staring at him, aghast at what he had done. Casey, more decisive, grabbed him by the collar and jammed a hand over his mouth.

He fought his way free. "What are you trying to . . .?" he began, and stopped as his voice boomed out once more.

From behind there came a loud cry. The long halloo of the hunter. It was immediately echoed by similar cries. A ring of voices sounding from all points of the compass.

"Fool!" Blossom was saying. "Fool!" Mouthing the same word repeatedly, her face pale with rage.

He felt a squirming movement in his pack, and the child had ceased to be a burden. All at once it weighed so little that when the others set off at a run he caught up with them easily. He felt as if he were being buoyed upwards, his feet passing effortlessly across the churned snow. Even Casey soon began to tire, whereas he, Tom, had energy to spare; and only Blossom, dragging at his arm, prevented him from taking the lead.

Directly ahead, a dark figure rose against the blank screen of the horizon. He veered aside, but not so Casey. Using both fists as a bludgeon, he struck the figure down. It was a harsh and brutal blow, yet when he turned to wave them on, his face showed none of that harshness. He wore a hurt expression and was clearly troubled by what he had just done.

Again they were running, the combined voices of the companions lifting in unheard song: a high-pitched vibration that soared above the clamour of pursuit. "Take care!" they urged him. "Care!" And he responded by conserving his energy, slowing down enough to stay within the protective circle of their bodies.

They were on a downhill slope now, and the horizon, previously so blank, wavered and shifted mysteriously. The cause of the mystery was soon apparent as shreds of mist swept raggedly past them. It thickened within moments, rising like steam from the unbroken surface of the snow; deadening their footfalls; swathes of it winding about them, hiding them even from the sky.

With the coming of the mist, the landscape had altered. They had entered a region of chaos, the ground no longer smooth, but compressed into ridges and inclines. Frozen boulders loomed above them; murky crevasses opened at their feet; between swirls of mist they spied dark gullies and even darker entrances to caves or lairs.

Gazing warily about him, Tom was reminded of a photograph he had seen once, of pack-ice in the southern oceans. Shrouded in a haze of mist, that too had looked like a region of madness: an endless jumble of twisted icefloes torn and worried by the currents beneath.

No sooner had he acknowledged the memory than the child changed its position, and seconds later the earth trembled, making Tom and his companions stagger and fall. It was as if the ground itself were unstable; as if it had somehow been transformed into the pack-ice of the photograph and was being torn by the same invisible forces.

The trembling motion had also disrupted the distant cries, though not for long. They were soon heard again, closer than ever. As Tom picked himself up and laboured on, another of the dark figures showed above the broken blossoms of ice that hemmed him in. No faceless pursuer, but someone he recognised: a fellow climber from a former life. There was nothing elfin about her. She appeared to him as he had always known her: a young plain-faced woman, her features unaffected by this frozen realm. He even remembered her name.

"Helen," he said aloud, his voice a tongue of flame that burned a clear passage through the mist. "Helen Fairchild."

"Tom . . .?" she began, and was cut short as Casey leaped forward and swung at her, his clenched fist clubbing her to her knees. She rose and was struck again, a glancing blow that sent her reeling away. Incredibly, she stayed on her feet, and then she was running for all she was worth, vanishing back into the mist.

Casey was about to follow when Blossom grabbed at him. Urgent words formed on her lips: "Not you! Not us! Them! Them!"

Even while he hesitated, two of the companions plucked short-handled cudgels from their packs and ran off.

"All!" Blossom insisted, and shook Casey with both hands. "All!" Her throat distended, straining against the silence that enclosed her.

Casey nodded reluctantly, and the rest of the companions broke away, clawing at their packs as they ran.

From somewhere beyond the wall of mist there was a noise of conflict: loud cries accompanied by the clash of weapons; and high above the turmoil, a voiceless song.

"They're trying to kill Helen!" Tom burst out, and the mist peeled back as before, parting to reveal a hazy drama, a vague shadow-play of action. "We have to stop them!" he added, and would have rushed into the fray had the clouds not swooped low and blanked out the scene of battle.

In the sudden obscurity Tom found himself confronted by Blossom and Casey. Arms linked, they stood directly in his path. He faltered, held there not just by their determined stance, but also by their faces – by their weird likeness to his own. A likeness so compelling that it occurred to him suddenly that within this strange realm he no longer belonged with people like Helen. He had been set apart from them from the moment he had stared into the petrified mirror of the cliff and seen elfin features peering out at him.

To ensure there was no mistake, he dragged off a glove and touched his face; let his hand move from the unnaturally long chin, up past the raised cheek-bones, to the pointed tip of one ear. I am the Carrier, he thought distinctly – familiar words that both confirmed and dulled his fears. Then he turned and scrambled away through the shattered landscape.

He broke from the mist some time later, out into a day already stained with the onset of dusk. His exposed hand had become frozen and lifeless, and he had to beat it against his side to bring back the feeling. His discarded glove was still hanging from a cord at his wrist, and he slipped it on over tingling fingers. By then Blossom and Casey had caught up, Blossom's face now greyer than the waning day, from the long run.

They crouched together in the fading light, catching their breath and waiting. On the brink of night they heard rapid footsteps and stood up, ready, Casey moving forward to defend them; but the person who staggered from the mist was merely one of the companions. Her weapon, her cap and gloves, were all gone. Teardrops had frozen to her cheeks and there was blood on the pale front of her jacket. Her face contorted by grief, she sank to her knees and pointed back over the way she had come – a simple gesture that revealed for the first time how withered her arm was, the hand convulsed into a deformed claw.

Tom recognised her at that moment – her also – and had almost recalled her name when Blossom intervened.

"Did you end her waking?" she demanded of the girl. Not in words. The question conveyed by the high song.

The girl shivered and gave he answer in mime: by

55

hunching over like a wounded bird and hobbling brokenly across the ice.

"So Helen's alive!" Tom cried out with relief. "She's still alive!" And the breath from his lips made the wall of mist part briefly, like a door swinging open and closed upon some ghostly presence.

Beside him Blossom punched aimlessly at the snow, her face impassive so it was impossible to guess at her true feelings. "Finish it!" she commanded, mouthing the words this time.

The girl let out a faint bird-cry of despair, her withered arm upflung, and in that instant Tom remembered her name. Before he could call to her, however, she had disappeared once more into the mist.

Bonny! he thought helplessly. That's who she is! Bonny Fairchild! She and Helen! Sisters! The two of them on opposing sides! About to meet in a last and terrible . . . !

He was protected from the full horror of that imagined scene by the clamour of the child. Its small hands scrabbled at his shoulders, distracting him, and with a grumble of discontent (or was it warning?), the ground trembled more violently than before. Down on all fours he could feel the rending and grinding of brittle surfaces far below, and in the forefront of his mind he saw again the photograph of the pack-ice. The whole frozen scene was in full motion, with huge sections of blue-white flow heaving skywards only to split or shatter in a spray of icy shards.

He waited, and as the surrounding ice settled at last he was dragged to his feet by Casey and Blossom. Head cocked to one side, he listened hard, but the distant conflict had ended. Helen, he suspected, and Bonny as well, were both lost to him by now. As locked in the past as the day itself.

He looked up dejectedly. Except for a pale band of blue, low on the horizon, the sky had turned a dense black. The only light came from the gleaming phosphorescence of the snow: a spectral glow barely strong enough to guide his footsteps as he turned and stumbled off into the gloom.

The place of sanctuary, when they came upon it, was unmistakable. Not a cave this time, but a deep crevasse. A negative image of Tower Rock that plunged straight downwards into nothing, its polished sides festooned with crystals of glittering frost. Peering over the edge, Tom could see where the crystals had gathered into a sparkling ledge or couch that hung poised above the abyss. Before he could draw back, the earth trembled yet again, and Casey, crouched near by, was pitched into space. Mouth stretched wide in a silent scream, arms and legs flailing, he was swallowed by the void. Tom very nearly followed him, but Blossom grasped at the straps of his pack and held on long enough for him to find hand and footholds.

Clinging onto nobs of crystal, he worked his way down, his own elfin image mirroring his every move. Once on the ledge, he slipped off the pack and placed it gently at his feet. The child's face, protruding above the flap, had never appeared more vulnerable. The swell of its forehead, fringed with golden hair, looked as fragile as the finest porcelain; its blue-veined temples throbbed with a secret life that totally denied the starkness of its surroundings.

"How can I leave you here?" Tom murmured aloud.

And from the crystal shapes all about him there came an answering hum of song: "Make haste! Make haste!"

He glanced up, and Blossom's lips shaped the self-same message. While from the deeps of the wintry land itself was heard a final growl of warning.

It was the low earth-voice that prompted him to act. Taking the axe from his belt, he drove it into the wall of the crevasse. Then he uncoiled the rope, looped it through a metal ring on the pack, and tied it securely to the axe-handle.

The child responded with a characteristic movement. Working one arm free, it let its half-cupped hand fall onto the frozen shelf, its dimpled knuckles settling beside a razor-edged bloom of crystal. "Look," it seemed to be telling him. "Here I am immune from all harm." It sighed contentedly, clenching its tiny fist. Immediately there was an answering jolt somewhere in the darkness of the earth, and Tom, who had been perched on the lip of the shelf, was flung backwards.

It was his worst nightmare. A fall from the heights. The void plucking him clear of the cliffs, the crevasse, the Tower – everything he had ever thought to climb. He looked up, agonizingly, to where Blossom was spiralling down to meet him. And knew in that instant that whatever his waking self should tell him, his fate and hers – their very hearts – were bound to each other. Always. He stretched out, straining to reach her, and their hands, gloveless, touched warmly palm to palm. With a quick compulsive movement, their fingers interlaced, held for a long moment, and then, at the very last, slipped slowly apart.

8 He slipped out of the house on the last stroke of six, with the sky overhead turning from dawn-pink to blue.

"Make haste, Tom," his mother called after him. "You don't want to be late on your first morning."

With a wave of the hand, he joined the steady stream of workers moving down the street – men and women in dingy jackets and caps and heavy boots that clattered on the cobblestones – all of them making for the mill. As he strode along amongst them he picked up snatches of conversation, murmured comments that stirred shadowy ghosts in his memory.

"The word is, there are four more this morning," he heard one man say. "Two of them those Fairchild girls. Sleeping like the dead they are, the same as the others."

"It's a bad business," a woman answered. "Even the doctors are baffled, and no wonder. It doesn't sound natural to me."

"You're right there. The Devil's handiwork, that's what I'd call . . ."

Tom, who had heard enough, was already moving on ahead, hurrying along the narrow streets towards the heavy iron gates of the mill. Just before he reached them he spied someone signalling to him: a poor match-seller, an open tray of matches suspended from his shoulders. At Tom's approach he smiled, his eyes crinkling up, narrowing, lifting at the corners . . . and straight away Tom recognised him as one of the companions.

Here in the waking day he looked older, in his early twenties perhaps, and he was unnaturally thin. His chest heaved at every breath and his lips were stained an unhealthy bluish colour. Under the pretext of selling Tom a box of matches, he drew him into furtive conversation.

"The older sister's still amongst us," he muttered, glancing suspiciously at a knot of passing workers.

"Older sister?" Tom queried uneasily.

"Helen Fairchild, the one who saw your face. Who knows who you are. We couldn't get to her, and now she's semi-conscious and likely to wake."

Tom experienced a strange mixture of feelings – relief and worry all jumbled together. "What if she *does* wake?" he asked.

There was a wheezy intake of breath and the bluish lips moved closer, the gasping voice more urgently confidential. "Why then they'll find out. She'll tell them who you . . ."

Someone pushed roughly between them – Blossom, her collar pulled up around her face. She did not attempt to speak. Her look alone was enough: a disapproving frown that told them clearly how risky it was to be seen together. So that when she turned aside and ducked down the nearest alley, the match-seller was not far behind.

Tom had little time to consider her warning. The whistle at the mill shrieked loudly, marking the end of one shift and the beginning of another, and he was caught up in a throng of jostling workers all hurrying to enter the gates. They dispersed quickly, leaving him alone in the dismal yard, surrounded on three sides by tall grey walls, the sky above stained with smoke from the mill's stacks.

All his life he had thought of this as a place to be avoided. "Go for a job in the open air," his father had advised him, hoping Tom would follow in his footsteps as a fisherman. Even when Tom had qualified for the hazardous career of climber, still his father had supported him. "Anything's better than the mine or the mill," he had reassured his wife. Yet here was Tom standing in the shadow of these bleak unlovely walls, cut off from the open spaces of cliff and sea; and more dreadful still, cut off also from the father who had supported and encouraged him.

The appearance of the night-shift interrupted his gloomy reverie. Grimy-faced, their shoulders slack with weariness, they trudged out into the yard, and Tom had to push through them to reach the main office. There, he was signed on and directed to a large inner door.

It swung open onto a great sombre cavern. A place of blistering heat and clanking noise, the air heavy with the smell of burning. After the brightness of the morning he could see almost nothing. Then the darkness was fractured by a cascade of light as one of the huge overhead ladles poured molten steel into a series of holding moulds. Somewhere further off there was a sharp crackle, followed by a strong whiff of sulphur, and flames and sparks spouted from a blast-furnace. Further off still, a continuous arrow of gold pierced the gloom, the result of white-hot ingots being fed through the rolling-mill.

Against these abrupt spasms of glare, dark shapes moved to and fro like shadowy puppets on an ill-lit stage. One of them took him by the arm and led him towards a roaring cauldron from which tongues of flame emerged periodically. Another figure appeared out of nowhere, larger and more familiar than the last; and Casey's face, neither friendly nor antagonistic, was gazing down at him, the soot-stained cheeks and forehead already running with sweat.

For the next few hours, half deafened by the constant turmoil, Tom had little idea of what was going on. He knew only that he was performing the heaviest work of his life. At Casey's direction he pulled at giant levers, slammed and locked others into position, while above him the blast-furnace raged noisily or poured forth its liquid gold – or, most spectacular of all, vented its tumbling heaps of glittering slag.

During a short lull in the work, as he leaned wearily against a shaft of hot metal, he felt he had stumbled into a kind of hell. Yet it was a hell of weird and wonderful sights, he had to admit that. A dusky cavern where beauty and ugliness met in an endless, unresolved conflict. Like . . . like what?

Another cavern, gleamingly beautiful, coldly empty, imprinted itself on the darkness before him. So briefly that he blinked and it was gone. And there was Casey back beside him, prodding him into action, making him wrestle with levers that controlled the roaring intake of air or emptied mounds of spent ash from the fire-boxes.

Through it all he kept thinking: Is this what it's going to be like for the rest of my working life? This? Long day- or night-shifts of smothering heat? Of deafening noise that left his head ringing? A breath of burning air caught him full in the face. So different from the cooling wind that blew in from the sea – the same wind and sea that had snatched his father from him. But wasn't even death on the open water preferable to this dungeon existence? A few hours of it was almost more than he could bear. How could he possibly endure it for the remainder of the day, and for all the hours and days that were to follow?

Fortunately for Tom he was never called on to answer that challenge. Above the combined din of blast-furnace and machinery, he heard his own name thundered accusingly.

"Tom! Tom Roland!"

It was a voice that could have belonged to only one man – Jack Steele! – and his presence at the mill could have meant only one thing: that the climber, Helen Fairchild, had woken from her coma and told them that he, Tom . . . that he . . .

His mind, perplexed by this sudden turn of events, balked at what it was being asked to do: to bring his waking and his sleeping selves into single hard focus.

"But I *am* the Carrier," he murmured aloud.

He had not intended to say that. The statement seemed to come to him of its own accord. As did the slight form that flitted towards him through the shadows.

Blossom, her dark outline as unmistakable as Jack's voice, snatched at his hand and drew him away from the glare of an erupting furnace. Perplexed still, he tried to hold back, but Casey was at his other shoulder, pressing him forward.

"They're onto you!" he explained urgently, his mouth brushing Tom's ear. "They know who you are!"

As if to prove Casey's point, Jack's shout rang out again. "Tom? Can you hear me, Tom?"

There was an unrelenting quality about the voice that made Tom cringe away, and he followed Blossom more readily now. To where a loop of chain dangled almost to the floor.

At Blossom's bidding he grasped it firmly and was winched upwards as Casey dragged hand-over-hand at the other side of the loop. The murky upper portion of the mill rose to meet him: a bewildering criss-cross of steel girders, and above them the zigzag pattern of the roof. He stepped onto the nearest girder and was joined first by Blossom, and a little later by Casey who had hauled himself up by brute strength.

From their raised vantage point they had a wide view of the mill floor. Like the grotto of some nameless ogre, it spat fire at them, with great pockets of darkness exploding into gaudy light and then subsiding. Between the flash and dazzle of flame and molten metal, tiny figures scurried about, searching into the farthest corners.

"It's no good hiding, Tom." Jack's voice again, louder and more demanding. "We'll get you in the end."

One of the searching figures had stopped beside the

swinging loop of chain and was stalling up towards them. Silently, Blossom motioned with one hand and they clambered away through the forest of girders, their path lit partly by the fires below, partly by the occasional smoke-blackened window set into the roof.

"Listen to reason, Tom," the voice called. "You're fooling yourself if you think you can escape. The only way out of here is straight past me."

A ladle directly beneath them was slowly upended, and in a brief dazzle of light Tom saw that what the voice claimed was true. Jack himself was standing squarely in the wide exit from the mill. There was a second brilliant sunburst, and Tom also noted that more than one person had followed them up the chain. Several stealthy forms were now gliding between the girders, each with a glint of metal in one hand.

"I'll make a bargain with you, Tom," Jack called enticingly. "Give yourself up and your friends will come to no harm. You have my word on that."

A bargain, Jack called it, but what alternative was there? The only exit was blocked, and a ring of armed figures was closing in steadily.

Half-decided, Tom glanced towards Blossom. She shook her head as if able to read his thoughts. Taking off her jacket, she handed it to Casey and pointed to where a smudge of daylight showed through the roof. He seemed to understand her purpose because he wrapped the jacket about his fist and punched at the glass pane which shattered into fragments, leaving behind a square of clear blue. Seconds later they were free, standing on a steeply sloping section of roof, the spring sunlight pouring down onto their upturned faces.

Only now, with the wind cool against his cheek, did Tom realise how hot and trapped he had felt in the stifling gloom below. This unexpected escape was like a release from hell – a hell of weird and unsettling beauty. He leaned back, eyes closed, and took a grateful breath of fresh clean air.

This was no place to linger, however. Jack's voice, still audible through the open window-space, was egging his followers on; and nearer at hand Blossom was trying to attract Tom's attention with a series of strangled cries.

On all fours he scrambled up to where Casey and Blossom were waiting, and one behind the other they hurried along the narrow line of the ridge. At the first valley, where two different angles of the roof met, they slid down feet first, digging in their heels so as not to overshoot the edge.

They had reached the blind side of the building, the ground below crossed by a railway line which brought coal in from the mine. There was a train down there now, its trucks being emptied onto a conveyer-belt which in turn deposited the coal at the top of a growing black heap.

"This side's no good," Casey said. "It's too open."

Only Blossom disagreed. Pointing to the train, to show what she had in mind, she moved along the edge of the roof to where a cast-iron drainpipe ran all the way to the ground.

For all three of them it was an easy climb. Once down they had only to dash across a fringe of asphalt to the last of the empty trucks. As they clambered inside, the train lurched into motion and trundled towards the distant viaduct that curved around the upper end of the valley.

Crouched in the dusty interior they thought that at last they were safe, for the time being anyway, but just before they left the mill grounds a lookout on the roof sang out a warning.

"The train! They're in the train!"

Footsteps pounded along beside the line. There was a soft thud as someone leapt onto the truck. Two hands appeared on the upper lip, followed by a man's face. "Here . . . !" he began to yell, but Casey punched at his hands and he fell back. Other footsteps took up the chase, further off, fainter, soon dying away as the train gathered speed.

Casey, his features blurred by a rising haze of coal dust, was grinning triumphantly, but Tom was more pensive. He knew Jack would be contacting the mine by now, so that was no refuge; and the streets of the town, even the open countryside, would be just as hazardous in broad daylight.

He looked questioningly at Blossom. She was standing up in the swaying truck, listening. Tom also listened, and heard a change in the note of the wheels as the train braked and rumbled more slowly onto the viaduct. It was what she must have been waiting for. Gesturing for Tom and Casey to follow, she scrambled over the side of the truck and slipped down onto the track.

They were at a point where rows of terraced houses crowded against the viaduct. A short jump and they had landed on the nearest roof. The slates, brittle with age, cracked beneath them and slid noisily into the gutters, yet they never once paused. Bent low so nobody could see them from the street, and with Blossom leading, they ran along the inner slope, leaping the gap where one line of terraces ended and another began. Twisting and turning, observed only by the incurious birds, they threaded their way through the town until they came to a row of taller, more stately houses.

Again a drainpipe served their purpose. Once at the top, they crossed to a skylight which lifted easily, giving them access to a sun-streaked attic. Its trapdoor, too, was unlocked, and like three dishevelled thieves they descended a ladder to the main body of the house – a sombre place, its passageways decorated with old-fashioned wallpapers and equally out-of-date gas-fittings.

No one challenged them until they reached the ground floor. Then a door opened, a heavy baize curtain was swept aside, and the angular figure of a middle-aged woman stepped out into the passage. Like the rest of the house, her clothes looked curiously old-fashioned: her cap, her fingerless gloves, the high collar of her blouse, were all made of the finest lace; while her voluminous skirt reached right down to the floor. She did not seem at all surprised to find them there. Even their filthy appearance failed to unsettle her.

"Yes?" she asked distantly.

Casey wrenched off his cap and limped forward, his eyes lowered respectfully. "Sorry for intruding on you, ma'am," he muttered, "but we've brought the Carrier. We had to. They've found out about him."

Only her eyebrows moved. "I see," she said, as though everything were clear. "In that case you'd better wait for my husband. He'll know what to do."

"Your husband?" Tom asked.

"Why Mr Crawford," she answered, and smiled knowingly at him. "Who else?"

*   *   *

Having eaten a good meal and washed off the grime of the morning, they spent the rest of the afternoon hiding in the attic. For Tom it was a particularly frustrating time because try as he might he could get nothing out of Blossom or Casey. Blossom merely glowered at him, and Casey met all his questions with the same reply: "Ask Mr Crawford."

He was not given the chance to do so until early evening. As the skylight darkened above them, they heard the front door open and close, and soon afterwards Mrs Crawford summoned them downstairs.

They were shown into a room at the back of the house. It had an air of secrecy about it, of being closed off from the rest of the world. The only window was heavily curtained, and the gas lamp had been turned down so low that it seemed to cast as much shadow as light. Mr Crawford, still in his smart daytime suit, was standing with his back to the empty hearth, as if cold were his natural element and he was somehow able to take comfort from the blackened grate.

"Welcome, friends," he murmured, and presented

67

them with a blank gaze as his glasses mirrored the soft glow of the lamplight.

Tom did not bother with pleasantries. "I need to know what's happening to me, Mr Crawford," he said quietly.

The reply carried an edge of reprimand. "But you have the Dream. For you it has become a reality. Isn't that enough?"

The Dream! Now, as always, he was able to conjure only fragments of it: a sleeping face, a wilderness of ice and snow, the menacing cry of a hunter. The moment he tried to draw those fragments together, to fit them into a sequence of events, they dissolved like shadows in the sunlight.

"Maybe it would be enough if I could remember it properly," he complained. "The trouble is, it starts to fade as soon as I wake up. All I'm left with are bits and pieces."

"The child then," Mr Crawford added in the same tone of mild reproval. "You've had the privilege of seeing it. Of holding it in your arms. Of feeling its strange power. Surely that should satisfy you."

Did it? As he pondered the question, the elusive beauty of the child's face came back to him, its eyelids quivering in silent appeal. An appeal that it pained him to refuse.

"I need to know a lot more than that," he insisted stubbornly. "Such as who the child is, and why Jack's been after me today."

"You ask a great deal," Mr Crawford answered, his long face half-turned away.

"Doesn't the Carrier have that right?" Tom challenged him.

The lamplit moons of the glasses swept back towards Tom. For several seconds a struggle seemed to go on behind them. Then a chilly friendliness broke through in a half-smile.

"Forgive me," Mr Crawford said. "I'm only trying to protect you. Too much knowledge, you must realise, can be as destructive as too little. But you're right. As the Carrier, you at least deserve to know . . ."

There was a hiss of warning from Blossom, which stopped him in mid-sentence.

"Tell him the story, Mr C," Casey said hastily. "He'll like the story."

Tom whirled around, but both Casey and Blossom had withdrawn into the darkest corner. And when he turned back, Mr Crawford was gazing at him with the same chilly friendliness as before.

"Aah yes, the story," he whispered, and his voice had suddenly become more intimate, as secretive as the room itself. With a sigh, he settled into the nearest chair. "I won't begin it in the usual way. Not with 'Once upon a time', because this isn't a fairy story, Tom. It's about a very real past. I'll ask you instead to imagine a period before books and writing were ever thought of; and also before wars and hardship and grubby little towns like this had come into being. A golden age of ancient wisdom and enduring beliefs. Let your mind drift back towards it, and then picture to yourself a peaceful settlement on this very shore. Not a grand city, full of finery and show. A settlement – just that – inhabited by families of fisherfolk and farmers, and by a few poor scholars steeped in the old ways. A timeless place full of beauty and grace, where the wisdom of one generation is the wisdom of every other. Where people live as their parents lived before them." His voice dropped lower, became even more intimate as he leaned forward in his seat and fixed Tom with his gaze. "Where each and every child rests secure in the knowledge that a loved father will never be snatched away when he's needed most. Can you picture it, Tom?" he asked challengingly. "Your own father sailing back into harbour? Can you? In your mind's eye? Or there, in the glow of the lamp?"

He paused, and in the lull Tom looked deep into the soft ball of gaslight – so deep that the surrounding streets, the smoke-blackened buildings of the town, seemed to vanish, leaving him on an unspoiled sunlit shore, staring hopefully out to sea. To where a familiar boat – yes, he could almost see it! – was butting against the outgoing tide, drawing ever nearer.

Mr Crawford nodded understandingly. "Now let me ask you to imagine something more," he went on in his husky whisper. "Not a place. Not someone you have known and loved, but someone higher still. No less a person than the ruler of this ancient settlement. A man neither young nor old, because he has always been here. A man who is all-powerful, and yet as humble as the lowliest of his subjects; all-wise, and yet wedded to simplicity. He has no throne, Tom, no glittering palace. And do you know why? Because his true home is the heart of his people. Come what may, it is the one place from which he can never be removed. Even now he lurks in all our hearts. Yes, Tom, yours too. He is a part of us still, ready to lead us out of these darker, more desperate days."

Again he paused, allowing the meaning of his words to take effect. In the lengthening silence, Tom looked up at the clock on the mantelpiece, but it had stopped. Its glass was yellow with age, both hands locked together on the twelve.

"What I have told you so far is the eternal story," Mr Crawford murmured. "But there is also a temporal story. One far easier for an age like ours to imagine. Would you hear that too?"

Tom nodded, saying nothing.

"Very well. Then picture now a group of very different men and women who have grown like a cancer in the midst of our peaceful settlement. People hungry of heart, infected by jealousy and ambition. People dedicated to the wrack and torment of time, who believe that only through change, through what they foolishly call history, can humanity find fulfilment. What do you think such restless beings would do to our changeless haven here on these quiet shores?"

"They'd destroy it," Tom answered.

Mr Crawford nodded sadly. "That is in fact what they *tried* to do. The settlement they took by force, and its inhabitants they enslaved. Believe it or not, we are the descendants of those slaves, Tom. But what was done to us was the least of evils. These destroyers!" He spat the word out. "They also moved against the ruler. Unable to kill him, for that was beyond their power, they took his body – only his body, Tom – and they locked it in a rocky cell, where they fondly believed it would never be found. As for his spirit, that they banished to the world of sleep."

"Sleep?" Tom exclaimed. "But that's fantastic!"

"Is it? Think back to your childhood. To the stories passed on to you by your parents. Ancient legends of men or women who slumber on for years. You must have heard them. Stories like Sleeping Beauty, which tell of fabulous beings who can be roused from their age-long sleep only with a loving kiss. Well, our ruler is the first and greatest of those sleepers. He is the root of all such legends. Except that in his case far more than a kiss is required to break the spell that binds him. If he is to wake, some hardy soul must rescue his banished spirit and carry it back to that secret place where dream and reality become one and the same."

"The Carrier!" Tom muttered, half to himself.

"Precisely, Tom," Mr Crawford agreed, speaking so softly that the words seemed to insinuate themselves into Tom's mind. "You, as the Carrier, are the chosen one. The one destined to free the Sleeper from his trance by bearing his spirit-self through the wastes of the Dream to where he lies hidden and waiting. No easy task, as you've already found out. For the envious, the unbelievers, the hungry of heart are always with us, and they will stop you if they can. Either in the here and now, or in that dream world through which you must carry your precious charge."

Tom glanced up, struck by a sudden thought. "You said the Sleeper was a man. Well, he isn't. He can't be.

71

His banished spirit, if that's what you call it, is a child. A sleeping child!"

"Is that so surprising?" Mr Crawford answered easily, and leaned back until Tom could see his half-closed eyes behind the glasses. "Dreams often show us things as they truly are. And within the Dream world, what is the Sleeper's lost spirit but a helpless child? A child severed from its larger self? It is for you, Tom, to empower them both. To bear the infant spirit to that rocky cell where his adult body has lain imprisoned for ages past. Only there can the child and the man unite into one whole being. Into the ruler of old, awake at last, and ready to defeat his enemies."

"This cell or prison," Tom asked curiously, "where is it?"

Immediately the glasses flashed, while from the darkened corner Blossom sounded another low hiss of warning. Like a breath of cool air, it seemed to unsettle the stillness of the room.

"You are asking things only the Sleeper can answer," Mr Crawford said evasively. "Rest assured that if you trust him, he will guide you there. Trust, that's what he expects of you, Tom."

"But why me?" Tom objected, sensing that something was being withheld. "Why have I been chosen?"

Mr Crawford cleared his throat uncomfortably. "I won't lie to you, Tom. You weren't our first choice. Originally Blossom was going to be the Carrier, but that was before . . . before . . ." He coughed again and beckoned her from the corner. "See for yourself. Look at what they did to her. After this, you were our best hope."

Tom turned towards Blossom, but as always it was not her damaged body that he saw. It was her face, her eyes: so darkly watchful, so coldly attractive, that they told him little. What was she feeling now? he wondered. Shame? Outrage? Resentment that he, Tom, should have taken her place?

"I . . . I'm sorry," he stammered, unsure of what else to say to her.

She shrugged off his concern, acting as if all he were offering was pity.

"She has Jack Steele to thank for her injuries," Mr Crawford pointed out. "He's the one to blame. Higher and higher he drove her, not content until she fell. He wanted to do the same to you, Tom, but you outfoxed him, by pretending you were afraid of Tower Rock." Leaning back in his seat, he let out a throaty chuckle. "Ah yes, you put him off the scent there."

"But I *am* afraid of the Rock," Tom admitted.

An awkward silence fell upon the room. Mr Crawford's mouth had dropped open, and Casey had moved out from the corner, his eyes wide with surprise. Blossom was the only one who appeared unperturbed, the hint of a smile playing about her lips.

"Well ... er ... fear is ... er ... something we all have to ... er ... to deal with," Mr Crawford blustered. "And you will deal with it, Tom. You'll ... er ... you'll cope when the occasion arises. I'm sure of that."

He stood up to hide his agitation. "Time for us all to turn in, I think," he said briskly, trying to act light-hearted, and he ushered them towards the door. "Boring old sleep for me," he added, laughing, "and the great adventure for you."

At the foot of the stairs he became serious again, his mournful face lit by a sudden sense of yearning. "What I wouldn't give to trade places with you now," he murmured. "If only for this one night. What a privilege! To carry the child-spirit of the Sleeper. To safeguard it through the many hazards of the Dream. Aah, that would be something." He shook his head sorrowfully, and the pale gleam of the glasses fixed upon Tom. "I hope you're mindful of the honour bestowed upon you, lad. I hope, too, you can live up to it. Yes, indeed." And with a last breathy sigh, he left them to find their own way to the attic.

There, some half an hour later, Tom lay staring up at the scatter of stars which showed through the skylight. Although he was tired, he was not quite ready to exchange the security of these last wakeful moments for the uncertainties of the Dream. On either side his two companions were already asleep, Blossom's up-turned face softened by the dim light from the stars. Impulsively, he reached for her hand, and only then did he close his eyes. As he drifted off he wondered briefly why the Sleeper's Dream world contained no stars. And with that question came another: a query he had meant to put to Mr Crawford earlier. Why was it that within the Dream his own face took on the elfin likeness of the child? As did the faces of all the companions? Why . . . ?

9 The reflected face followed him up the side of the crevasse. Because of distortions in the glassy surface, the features were even less like his own: the chin and nose drawn to the finest of points; the tilted eyes picking up greenish tints from deep in the ice; the pupils oddly out of shape. He covered the image hastily with his mittened hand, but the moment he moved higher, there it was again, staring out at him. Himself, and yet not himself. An undiscovered identity that made him shiver and turn his head away.

Coming upon the child helped to allay his fears. Here the tiny elfin features conveyed an undeniable charm. He knelt beside it on the narrow ledge, wishing more than ever that it would wake and look at him. He had a vivid idea of what its eyes would be like: not a hard icy green, but soft and warm, as calm and welcoming as the summer sea. He reached down, intending to shake the child tenderly from its long sleep; to rouse it just enough for a glimpse of recognition to pass between them. But one dimpled hand shot out and clamped vice-like upon his wrist, holding him there powerless, while the glittering crystals, embedded in the surrounding walls, pierced him with their hard white beams.

He was not aware of being released. Or of strapping the child to his back. He had left the ledge and was climbing through bands of rainbowed light, up to where a sky of low cloud closed off the crevasse like a watchful grey eye. There were whitish flecks as its outer edges – the moon-pale faces of the companions gazing down at him. So few, he thought unhappily, for he could count only five. Yet their song

75

remained unchanged: high and joyful except for one discordant note which came from Blossom.

Casey, grinning a welcome, gripped his arm and hauled him up into a freezing cold day. The wind was blowing strongly, lifting the surface snow in a fine hail that stung his cheeks. The fiercest gusts tore at the nearby bank of mist, but failed to dispel it, and when the group resumed their journey, it hung down behind them like a billowing curtain, screening them off from anyone who might be following.

Their onward path lay directly into the wind, and with one hand raised to ward off the stinging particles, Tom peered ahead. Before him stood what seemed at first to be a vertical white wall. He blinked and refocussed, and the wall became an utterly featureless plain – or what would have been a plain if it had not been tilted slightly. In his very gloomiest moments he had never visualized anything quite so dull and monotonous. Nothing disrupted its even covering of snow; nothing, no drift or hillock, rose high enough to pierce the horizon and show where land and sky met. Near could have been far, and far just a few paces away. There was no means of telling. Wherever he looked the same off-white expanse stretched on and up into oblivion.

Its effect on the companions was instantaneous. Their song died to a whimper and they moved into a tighter formation, seeking comfort from each other. Even Blossom shrank in closer to the group. So close that when Tom stumbled under the weight of the child, it was she who reached out to steady him. He knew better than to thank her; he merely plodded on, grateful to have her at his side.

They had left the ragged bank of mist far behind. Now their only protection came from the haze of wind-blown snow. But it was poor cover, and despite their light-coloured clothing they were clearly visible against the drab background.

So too were the hunters when – as Tom knew they must – they finally appeared. As insignificant black dots to begin with, dark specks on either flank that somehow resisted the pressure of the wind; then as moving figures whose path was slowly converging with that of their prey. They did not raise their usual hallooing cries. Not this time. Silent and intent, they closed in steadily lifting their legs high as they churned through the drifts.

The companions were equally silent. Unnaturally so. Their song had dropped to nothing, and as they struggled to increase their pace even their gasping breaths were stifled. Minutes passed, and still the only sounds were the sighing of the wind and the faint crunch and squeal of compressed snow. It was as if hunters and prey had made a pact not to disturb the day; as if they had agreed in advance to this quiet but deadly game.

To Tom it made no sense. Earlier there had been a reason for silence. But now? When it was surely too late to avoid a violent conflict? For the converging figures were drawing dangerously near. Already he could almost see their faces. One of them, a man with a thick-set body and sturdy limbs, caused Tom to catch his breath in fright. A name, as dreaded as it was familiar, seemed to fall on him from the sky.

"Jack!" he broke out involuntarily. "Jack Steele!"

He had not expected an answer. Especially from the land. A shuddering rumble that halted him in his tracks; that brought him and everyone else to their knees, hunters and companions alike. The wind, the scudding clouds, stopped abruptly, as if in sympathy, and in the eerie stillness the last of the driven snow drifted slowly down.

As the air cleared, so a craggy pinnacle of ice rose before them, its summit vanishing into the cloud. Beyond it, and nearly half as high as the pinnacle, lay a vast bank of snow. Like a breaking wave, it stood on the point of collapse – thousands upon thousands of crystal tonnes teetering forward precariously. Great cracks criss-crossed it from top to bottom; dark caverns of emptiness undermined it. Only a miracle or some superhuman act of will prevented it from crashing down and smothering the plain.

"How did that . . .?" Tom began.

And the vibration of his voice, ominously loud in the crystalline air, produced another rumbling groan. The whole bank leaned outwards; the cracks widened; fresh caves yawned at its base. There was a second, softer groan, and then – a further miracle – the massive structure eased forward a fraction and settled, through it was balanced so delicately now that the slightest noise would have been enough to bring it tumbling upon the heads of those watching from below.

As yet no one had moved – no one had dared to – their eyes fastened on the overarching crest. Tom, ever mindful of the burden he carried, was the first to recover. Step by cautious step he began to walk backwards, feeling for his former footprints so as not to disturb the brittle surface snow; but the child had stiffened inside the pack, its body rigid with denial; and Blossom was shaking her head at him and pointing towards the pinnacle.

He understood at once that she was right. If they retreated, then even supposing they escaped the avalanche, the hunters would run them down on the open plain. Their one chance of real safety lay in reaching the pinnacle, in climbing above the level of the avalanche's breaking crest.

So began the deadliest part of the game. A silent race across the snow in the very shadow of destruction.

For the first few minutes it seemed that the companions must get there first; but then one of the hunters, faster than the rest, veered in and threatened to cut them off. At a curt nod from Casey, the girl to Tom's left turned aside to meet the challenge. She glanced back once, directly at Tom, and in a flash of recognition he saw her as she was: her eyes white and sightless. Blind? he thought wildly. Then how . . .?

He was distracted by another of the hunters crossing his line of vision. Casey nodded again, and this time the boy to Tom's right peeled off from the group. Unlike the girl he did not glance behind, but as he slipped free of his pack the upper part of his body was outlined against the snow, revealing one hunched and crooked shoulder.

Tom wanted to yell out for them to stop – to make a stand together, all of them – but the towering bank of snow creaked threateningly, silencing him; urging him on despite the sense of shame which followed like a shadow at his heels.

They were ahead of the hunters now. A small group of four. Then of three, as Casey nodded to the last of the companions, a wan-faced young man with bluish lips. Tom did not see him slow down, cudgel in hand, ready to guard their rear. He, Tom, was too busy racing for the base of the pinnacle, so consumed by the danger looming above that he could think of nothing else.

He reached the first of the outer ledges and scrambled onto it, his booted feet ringing sharply on the hard surface. Yet again the heaped snow made its complaint, a growled warning to him as he clambered rapidly from ledge to ledge. Casey and Blossom were not far behind: Blossom's laboured breaths further fracturing the silence; her high discordant song screaming at him beyond the pitch of hearing.

Together they began the vertical part of the climb. Following Tom's lead, they hauled themselves up knife-edged buttresses, swung hazardously from needles of ice, entrusted their lives to flimsy handholds. Under other circumstances they would have been awed, even terrified by the challenge of this spindly wind-worn structure, but not now. Their one thought was to put as much distance as possible between them and the ground, and to that end they took risk after risk, growing ever more reckless in their haste.

It was a minor mishap that brought Tom to his senses. A nob of ice snapped off beneath his weight, leaving him hanging by his hands. After the initial shock he knew he was in no real danger; but to Casey, immediately below and aware only of Tom's legs kicking free, it seemed he was about to fall.

"No!" Casey cried, his voice swelling out into the fragile silence.

The reverberations had hardly died away when there was a sharp crack, like a rifle going off, followed by a dreadful pause. Fleetingly, Tom looked across his shoulder, down onto the sloping plain, to where the warring groups showed as mere specks upon the snow: three dark circles of them, each with the pale figure of a companion at its centre. They were strangely still, as though poised, waiting. Then the circles broke apart and the combatants were scattering in all directions, like ants racing from some giant foot.

Tom never saw how many survived. A cold blast of air struck his cheek, and when he swung around the whole vast bank of snow was exploding outwards. The noise alone nearly shook him loose, but the impact was worse. As the weight of snow crashed down upon the plain, the shock-wave sent a tremor up the pinnacle that broke his hold and left him clutching at the air. Helpless, he slid down onto Casey and Blossom, and together they somehow managed to hang on. Seconds later the avalanche itself slammed into the pinnacle, bending it like a reed. The top portion, including the part where Tom had been climbing, snapped off and vanished. Vicious splinters of ice rained down. And Tom was alone again, grabbing for nonexistent handholds, gathering speed as he bumped from ledge to ledge; while far below the plain was blotted out, replaced by a furious white storm that seethed and foamed and roared.

The noise and turmoil seemed to go on for an unbearably long time. When at last it stopped, Tom found he was dangling in space, suspended by his shoulder-straps, one of which was looped around a finger-thin needle of ice. Even in his dazed state he recognised that so thin and fragile a piece of ice could not possibly hold the combined weight of him and the child. Yet it could! It did! What is more, it continued to support them until Casey's mittened hands closed about the shoulder-straps. As they were dragged to safety, two things happened: the child, which had been lying deathly still within the pack, its body rigid with concentration, let out a sigh of sleepy pleasure and relaxed warmly against him; and the needle of ice, relieved of its burden, snapped off and spun away.

With Casey's help he clambered up to the shattered summit where Blossom was waiting impatiently. At her insistence, he stripped off the pack and placed it in her outstretched arms. Her hands trembling with apprehension, she lifted the flap . . . and discovered to her relief that the child was unharmed. Its skin remained pink and unblemished; its halo of golden hair shone in the gloomy afternoon light. Impulsively, she bent forward and pressed her lips to its forehead, unable to hide either her relief or her surprise.

Tom felt no surprise, though. From the moment he had found himself dangling from that impossibly thin piece of ice, he had begun to appreciate fully the strange bond which existed between the child and this place. No natural hazard – not the searing cold nor the crazed might of an avalanche – was able to harm the tiny fragile body. Only the hunters could do that. Why, even the summit on which he now stood seemed designed to give the child comfort. For the top of the pinnacle, in snapping off, had left behind not a jagged, splintered stump, but a level surface. Mirror-smooth except for a few dazzling outcrops of crystal, it had at its very centre a cradle-shaped hollow which might have been deliberately fashioned.

Blossom resisted the urge to place the child there herself. Grudgingly, she handed it to Tom and half turned away, leaving him to complete the task. The child settled with its usual ease. As though from long habit, and with a breathy sigh, it flung out one half-cupped hand which rested gracefully against the side of its frozen nest.

His usefulness over, Tom straightened up and closed his eyes, fully expecting to be plucked from the pinnacle, out into the waiting void. The day was not yet spent, however, and when he re-opened his eyes nothing had changed. He was still perched on the summit, and Blossom was still there beside him, gazing miserably at the plain.

Minutes earlier, he had assumed that all her concern was for the child. Only now did he realise his mistake.

"Some of them have escaped," he said, and pointed into the near distance, where isolated specks moved against the snow.

She nodded, as grudgingly as before, and clutched her shoulders with both hands, struggling to contain her feelings. The tears came just the same, spilling onto her cheeks where they froze into tiny crystals that gleamed as brilliantly as any of those surrounding the child.

"Hush now," Tom whispered, echoing words a motherly voice had once spoken to him. How long ago? And why? He could not remember the reason. Just the ache of misery and loss. And he reached out for Blossom's trembling shoulders; drew her against him; held her there, barely mindful of Casey who looked on with puzzled eyes.

On no other occasion had he been quite so unwilling to leave this wasteland. So that when the summons arrived, he resisted it, trying to ignore the slowly darkening sky, the broad band of shadow that inched across the plain. It's not dark yet, he told himself stubbornly, holding onto Blossom. Not yet. Nor was it. But still the summons was there, too urgent to be denied. Tugging, wrenching at him. At him alone, for Blossom remained solid and real within the circle of his arms.

He threw back his head in silent protest and looked up at the sky. A black shape was imprinted there. So suggestive. Of what? What? Even as he allowed himself to wonder, he was taken.

10 From his makeshift bed on the floor, Tom looked up at the shape outlined against the dawn-grey skylight. It moved. Took on the likeness of a head and shoulders. Of someone turning their head this way and that in an attempt to penetrate the darkness below.

Tom's hand was still clasped in Blossom's. He tightened his grip and she was awake, as alert as he. Casey returned more slowly, and Tom had to jam a hand over his mouth to prevent him making any noise.

"Hunters!" he hissed into Casey's ear, the word occurring to him automatically, as if he were still caught up in the Dream.

No other warning was necessary. Hidden by the lingering shadows, they collected their few possessions, stole quietly down the attic ladder, and swung the trapdoor closed after them. They had barely done so when there was a sound of breaking glass as someone smashed in the skylight.

"This'll stop them for a while," Casey whispered, and he slid home the bolt on the trapdoor.

Mr Crawford, still in pyjamas and dressing-gown, was brewing tea in the kitchen. He glanced around, startled, as they entered. Without his glasses, his long face seemed longer, sadder, his eyes unexpectedly small and colourless.

"Are they here already?" he asked in a disappointed voice.

Casey jerked his thumb upwards. "They're stuck in the attic for the time being. I don't think they saw us."

Mr Crawford responded by clenching both bony fists. A flush of pink briefly stained the whiteness of his cheeks. "Damn!" he muttered angrily. "I was hoping for at least a day's grace." He coughed and brought his feelings under control. "Never mind, we're ready for them even now," he added, and taking a hurricane lantern from the nearest shelf, he lit it and led them through the kitchen to a door that opened onto the cellar.

From somewhere high in the house there was a splintering of wood; and almost simultaneously a heavy pounding at the front door. Mr Crawford half turned his head at each sound, but showed no further sign of anger or alarm. With the lantern held high, he guided them down a flight of steps and into a low-ceilinged room that ended with a blank wall.

Tom's first thought was that he had been tricked. Casey must have thought the same because he spun around, his face blank with dismay.

"I won't die like a rat in a trap!" he snarled. "Not for you or anyone. I'd rather . . ."

"Trust me, boy," Mr Crawford interrupted calmly, and pointed to where a large block of stone had been loosened in the wall. "There, that's your way out."

Shamefaced, Casey ran his fingertips along the gaps in the mortar. "I . . . I'm sorry, Mr C."

The older man lowered the lantern and his face became an eyeless mask. "I don't want your apologies, young Casey," he answered, handing him a crowbar. "All I need is your trust and the strength in that over-grown body of yours. Now let's see what you can do."

Eager to make amends, Casey thrust the crowbar into one of the narrow gaps beside the stone and heaved. The block slewed around and fell with a crash onto the floor, leaving behind a good-sized opening. Instantly the rank stench of the town sewer filled the room, making Tom gag and rear backwards.

"You can't ask us to go in there!" he said, appalled.

But it was not a question of being asked. Hurried footsteps clattered overhead, and Blossom snatched the lantern and ducked towards the opening. Just as she was about to disappear, Mr Crawford made a grab for her arm.

"What about the Dream?" he asked in an urgent whisper. "Were there any . . . any more . . . ?"

"It was bad last night, Mr C," Casey answered for her. "There may be one of ours left. It's hard to say."

"*One* left? Only one?" Mr Crawford looked suddenly stricken, his long face paler than ever despite the yellowish lantern light. "Which . . . which one?"

"Angus Hopetoun. He could have escaped. It's possible anyway."

"Ah; Angus," Mr Crawford sighed, slightly relieved. "In that case listen to me carefully. Stay out of sight for the rest of the day, and this evening try and get to the old mine where . . ."

He broke off as the cellar door burst inwards. Wordlessly now, his body shielding them from whoever was bounding noisily down the steps, he bundled Tom through the wall and pushed Casey after him.

They landed in ankle-deep water, in a tunnel whose walls and arched roof were constructed entirely of brick. The stench in there was indescribable. Tom, breathing in shallow gasps, was almost transfixed by it.

"Come on!" Casey whispered fiercely.

He tried to follow, but for the moment he was unable to move. All he could think of was how to get out of there. His hands were already groping at the slimy surface of the wall, feeling for the opening, when he heard someone shout his name aloud. So much anger, such accusation contained in that one word that he had no option but to turn and splash off after the bobbing, dancing lantern.

He was running slightly uphill, the water washing against his shins. Every so often he passed vaguely rounded shapes to his right or left, but he failed to register that they were side tunnels until he caught up with Blossom and saw them in the feeble light of the lantern. Blossom herself was tiring, her stooping run getting slower and slower. When eventually she stopped, there was no sign of pursuit: only a soft gurgle of water and the strangely muffled sound of tramping feet, from the early morning workers passing overhead. Listening to them, Tom let his eyes follow the direction of the sound, to where a fainter ring of light shone down onto the stream. With his sleeve pressed against his nose and mouth, he stumbled forward and pointed up at the daylight seeping in around the edges of a manhole.

"Here!" he whispered excitedly. "A way out!"

Blossom, more cautious than he, motioned him into one of the narrower side tunnels. There, they soon came upon another manhole, and with Casey to boost him up, Tom managed to lift it free and scramble out into the fresh clean morning.

They had emerged into a deserted side alley. It was an easy matter to saunter down from there and mingle casually with the crowd of workers passing along the main street. Dressed more or less like everyone else, and at that time of morning, they attracted little interest. To those around them they were just three more workers destined for the early shift at either mine or mill.

As on the previous morning, the general talk was all about the mysterious sickness that was striking people down.

"Hey, Artie," someone sang out. "Did anyone call on Dr Giles this morning?"

Artie, a pink-cheeked man with a cheery smile, did his best to look saddened by what he had to say. "There was three families waiting by the surgery when I passed," he answered promptly. "You could see from their faces what they were there for. That pinched, worried look they had about them."

"Aye, and chances are there are more families waiting at other surgery doors," a third voice joined in.

"An epidemic, that's what Dr Giles is calling it," Artie added enthusiastically, enjoying the attention he was receiving. "He was only telling me so last night."

"Get away!" a woman jeered. "Dr Giles wouldn't be talking to the likes of you."

"Would he not?" Artie retorted.

There was no opportunity for the argument to develop, because at that point the road divided, the mill workers going one way and the miners the other. Tom and his companions chose to stay with the miners, and only realized their mistake when it was too late, for without leather leggings and lamps and helmets, they stood out in the crowd. Now, for the first time, they attracted curious glances. A few of the miners nudged each other and pointed in their direction. Some even began to mutter aloud.

"Isn't that the lad Jack Steele's looking for?"

"Aye, that's him. Tom Roland by name."

"What's this about a reward for his capture? A sizable one by all accounts."

"A reward?" The word travelled rapidly through the crowd, halting some of those ahead.

There was a muttered warning from close by – "Step lively, young Tom" – and as a group of miners came at them, Tom and his companions set off at a run down the nearest side-street.

Here, in the upper portion of the town, on familiar ground, they soon shook off their pursuers in the maze of alleyways and dirt lanes that criss-crossed behind the houses. Again they were safe, yet for how long? At any moment someone might look out of a back window and recognise them, and then the chase would be on once more. What they needed was a sanctuary; somewhere to hide for the rest of the day.

To Tom, only one such place existed, and he led the way through a pattern of lanes to his own back gate.

Denny was playing on the kitchen steps when they entered the narrow yard. At the sight of Tom, he flew into his arms.

"It's Tom!" he shrilled, slipping free and running for the back door. "Tom's come home!"

There were footsteps on the stairs and Mrs Roland hurried into the kitchen. Tom expected her to rush forward and hug him as Denny had done, but instead she snatched Denny up and backed away.

"Where have you been?" she cried accusingly. "All night I waited up for you. I've been worried sick. Especially after the terrible things Jack had to say this morning."

"This morning?" he asked sharply. "So he's still alive!"

"Of course he's alive. Why shouldn't he be?"

Tom wasn't sure whether the news made him glad or sorry. "And he's been here, you say?"

She nodded, fighting to hold back tears. "Last night, and again soon after dawn. He says . . . he says how we mustn't go near you. How you're the Carrier and . . ."

"The Carrier?" Tom was immediately on his guard, but like Blossom, whose head had also jerked up with surprise, he had misunderstood.

"That's what he told me," Mrs Roland said tearfully. "You're carrying this terrible disease and . . . and you'll infect us all if we're not careful. The way you infected the poor lads and lasses lying like the dead in their beds."

She was crying openly now, still clutching tightly onto Denny; and when Tom tried to approach, she moved back, keeping her distance.

"I wouldn't hurt you or Denny, Ma," he said. "Honest to God."

"That's what I tried to tell Jack, but he knew I had Denny to worry about, not just you, and he talked me down. He went on and on about how dangerous you are. How you have to be stopped, for the sake of others. What on earth have you been up to, lad? What is there between the two of you?"

"It's a mistake, that's all," he said evasively.

"Then explain it to him. You know I'll back you up.

88

Tell him the truth yourself when he comes round this morning."

The mere mention of Jack's return sent Blossom scurrying towards the door. Casey, less easily alarmed, laid a hand on Tom's shoulder. "We can't stay here," he said.

"Take your hands off him, Casey Mallick!" Mrs Roland said hotly. "Leave him be!" Then to Tom, pleading with him now. "I've no idea what hold these two have over you. All I know is that you're my son and you need help. So don't shut me out, lad. Tell me what's happening. I'm begging you."

Tom dearly wanted to be open with her, but with Casey tugging at his shoulder and Blossom silently willing him to leave, he did not know where to start. There was such a lot to explain – the Dream, the child, the hunters, the Sleeper in his secret cell, Mr Crawford's impassioned talk of a golden past that could be recaptured if only he, Tom . . . if only . . . He shook his head. It was all too complicated. Also, stated baldly, it would have sounded too far-fetched. He wasn't even sure how much of it he believed himself. His one and only certainty was the child. Having held it in his arms, having witnessed the elusive beauty of its sleeping face, he felt tied to it; bound by cords of feeling that he could not break.

"I'm waiting, Tom," she prompted him.

He realized he had to tell her something, but he could not decide what. He looked at the way she was holding Denny so protectively, and all at once his mind was made up.

"How important is Denny to you, Ma?" he asked.
"What kind of question is that?" she flared back.

"Just answer me," he insisted. "Could you ever give him up, for anything at all?"

Her arms tightened around the child, drawing his face into the hollow of her neck. "You know I couldn't."

"Well that's how it is with me. There's . . . there's something I can't give up either. Not yet."

89

He saw her shoulders sag with defeat. "So you're running out on me," she said wearily.

"It's not like that . . ." he began, and was interrupted by Denny.

"Tom's not running away from us!" he cried, squirming free of his mother, and before she could stop him he dashed across the kitchen and threw his arms about Tom's neck. "You'll be coming back, won't you, Tom?"

"I will, Denny," he answered readily, and nodded to his mother to show she had nothing to fear.

"You promise?" Denny pleaded.

"I promise."

The childish face was pressed hard against his shoulder, the tiny hands holding onto him so tightly that it was almost like being back in the Dream. He half believed he was until Blossom plucked at his sleeve, recalling him to the present; and regretfully he disentangled himself. His mother, meanwhile, had given up all thought of keeping her distance. She was bustling about the kitchen, filling a canvas shoulder-bag with bread and apples and a thick wedge of cheese.

"Here," she said, and after handing him the bag, she drew his face roughly down to hers and kissed him on both cheeks. "Don't forget us, Tom," she said. "You're all we have."

He was too upset to answer. Clutching the bag to his chest, as though it were Denny or the elfin child, he hurried out to where Casey and Blossom were waiting.

Together, they crept stealthily along the back lane. Although they kept to the shadow of the fence, they had not gone far when a cry rang out and a dark figure stood up amongst the chimneys of a nearby rooftop. They doubled back, twisting and turning through the narrow byways – only to be sighted by another rooftop guard. Again they ducked and ran, and again they were spotted, the warning cries driving them further and further up the hillside, until soon they had passed the last straggly row of cottages and the open fell lay before them.

90

There were people waiting here, too: a long line of men and women advancing down the hillside to meet them, their booted feet trampling the young growth on the heather.

Casey, his fists bunched, was about to charge the line when Blossom shook her head and pointed over to their left. Not far away the blackened pit-head of the old mine rose against the sky. Abruptly, Tom recalled Mr Crawford's last urgent message: how they should try to get there by evening. Well, early or not, it was their one chance, and they sprinted across to it.

Close up, it was a drab, depressing place. The winding gear above the shaft was gone, leaving behind only the skeletal supporting structure; and most of the surrounding buildings had lost their roofs, their corrugated-iron walls either fallen in or half rusted away. It was from one of these buildings that someone called furtively to them, and when they stole inside, they were met by the same young match-seller who had waylaid Tom outside the mill. He was not dressed as a match-seller now: he wore the leggings and helmet of a miner.

"Angus . . . !" Casey began excitedly, and was silenced by a fiery glance from Blossom.

She was crouched by the door, peering out, to where the line of men and women had swung around to form a circle that completely enclosed the area of the pit-head. They were no longer hurrying, confident at last that they had their quarry trapped.

It was that confidence which gave Tom and his companions the time they needed. Time to light the safety lamps and put on the helmets Angus had brought for them. He had brought one other thing as well: a bright yellow canary in a tiny silver cage. Tom understood what such birds were for: to detect gas in the mine. He understood also that after years of neglect, there might well be pockets of gas in the old workings. Though right at that moment he was not thinking ahead: he was considering Angus himself. Suddenly the young man's bluish lips, his narrow chest and damaged lungs, made sense: once, when he was Tom's age perhaps, he must have been so badly gassed that he had never fully recovered. He had become one of the unlucky ones. Like all the rest of the companions.

All? Tom wondered uneasily. Did that include himself? But surely the loss of a father wasn't the same. It was a different kind of affliction altogether. Or was it? Casey hadn't thought so. A "handicap", he'd called it, "like losing your right hand" – those had been his very words. Well, was Casey right? Was Tom's grief merely another form of injury, one hidden from view? Had it left him any less crippled inside than, say, Blossom? Any less dissatisfied with the nature of his present life? With the town at large? Could it be that, in spite of his sound body, he shared with the other companions the same desire to . . .?

His train of thought was interrupted by a hoarse summons from Casey, and hastily he tied his safety lamp to his belt and joined the others at the door.

In the gaps between the buildings he could see how the circle of hunters was tightening – grim-faced men and women, whom he had known on the cliffs, drawing steadily closer. Closer still was the pit-head itself. A quick dash, their boots crunching on the asphalt, and the four fugitives were there, standing where years before the winding gear had lowered heavy cages into the depths. Now, apart from the rusty supporting girders, there was only a gaping hole in the ground, with the top of a wooden ladder showing above one edge.

Urged on not just by Casey, but by Jack's bull-like roar in the background, Tom swung himself onto the ladder . . . and almost fell as the top rung came away in his hands. He was more careful after that. Ignoring Blossom's impatient sighs, he tested each rung before putting his weight on it, descending slowly but surely into the damp and musty darkness.

At the first stage, he looked up at the square of blue high above, where Casey was fending off an attacker.

92

The man fell back, and Casey plunged recklessly downwards, his feet setting up a *rat-tat-tat* rhythm as they struck the rungs. "Keep going!" he yelled, and Tom reached across to the second ladder and resumed his own more cautious descent.

Soon he was completely dependent on his lamp, climbing down through a bubble of pale light that shone dully on the water-stained planking of the shaft. Grey-furred spiders clung to the rotted planks, their clusters of eyes gleaming like jewels; the whiskered heads of rats, beady-eyed, peeped out at him suspiciously; icy-cold droplets smacked against his cheeks when he lifted his face to the three lights strung out above him.

Beyond the lights he could make out a line of dark forms following them down. Always, if he gazed up, they were there, rarely more than a ladder's length behind. He was so busy checking on their progress that the sudden feel of solid ground beneath his feet caught him unawares. "I'm down!" he called, and stepped clear as his companions came tumbling after him.

There was blood on Casey's face and a grim determination about him that Tom had never seen before. "Get out of here," he said shortly. "All of you." And grasping the ladder with both hands, he wrenched at it, struggling to pull it free of the wall.

Tom did not wait to witness the outcome. Spurred on by the cries of fear coming from the shaft, he set off along the low-ceilinged tunnel. Behind him there was a cracking noise as the ladder broke away, and quickly he blocked his ears against the thud of falling bodies.

That was why he did not hear Angus's breathless yelp of warning. He glanced around, thinking that Angus and Blossom were there at his shoulder, and found he was alone. His the only light in that part of the tunnel. The lights of his companions already far behind.

He stopped, aware now of their distant voices. They sounded strangely muffled, their words reaching him in uncertain fragments. " . . . unsafe!" they were yelling. " . . . the bird! . . . the bird!"

His head felt fuzzy. Heavy. What were they yelling about? Bird? What bird? Ah yes, the canary. He remembered it now, a bright chirruping creature which they had brought down here to warn them . . . warn them . . . Of what? And why had the bird grown so silent? Unless . . . Unless . . .

Too groggy to think clearly, he needed several moments to make the necessary connection. Then he began to run back over the way he had come, his hands reaching out desperately, as if trying to grasp the distant balls of light. Somehow they eluded him. Bobbing like will-o'-the-wisps, they slipped through his groping fingers, grew ever fainter, more tantalizing, and finally winked out altogether as his legs gave way and he slumped unconscious onto the sodden floor.

11 He slumped to his knees on the floor of the entrance and peered fearfully into the uncertain night. What could have made such a terrifying cry? Neither wholly human nor animal – more terrible than both – it had stopped him just as he was about to step across the threshold. Now, hesitant, he scanned the blackness of the sky; searched the tumbled snow on which a fresh skim of frost glimmered dimly. As far as he could tell, nothing moved out there. Nothing had changed. The surrounding landscape, battered by the avalanche, was just as he had left it. What remained of the pinnacle was as fairly rooted as ever. Icily pure, a fitting resting place for the child, it arrowed up from the plain, immovable.

Immovable?

Tom listened and heard a distant murmur of thunder. A faint tangle of lightning played across the horizon. And in response to those far-off signals, the whole pinnacle seemed to tremble slightly. He inspected it more carefully. Had it really moved? Or had he just imagined it? After all, the only light came from the snow itself, a pale greenish luminescence that gave to everything a sense of unreality.

Undecided, he lingered there at the threshold. Waiting. Not yet daring to enter this trackless waste alone. Especially at night. When it was haunted by strange cries.

The thunder sounded once again, much closer. The resultant lightning shone brighter, a distinct flash. And yes! This time he was certain. The pinnacle did move. Like an icy cord stretched between earth and sky, it vibrated and gave off a high thin note. Almost a wail, as though the land were alive and suffering grief.

But why should it grieve? And for what?

Above him the blackness of the sky deepened, coiled in upon itself, and finally erupted into racing stormclouds. As they massed and boiled, the thunder and lightning occurred almost together – an ear-splitting explosion, a dazzle of sheer brilliance. Flash after flash followed, the noise deafening; forked paths of light fractured the dark. One, a lightning bolt of great intensity, struck the pinnacle and shook it to its foundations. In that split-second of total illumination, a horrifying figure was revealed, standing astride the summit. A figure which partly resembled a huge bird of prey, with horned beak, taloned feet, and bony jutting wings; partly, too, it was like some fabulous beast, its long muscular body ending in a lashing tail. And its eyes! A bright electric green, the elongated pupils flecked with red, they glared furiously out over the plain.

Tom caught the merest glimpse of the creature, but that was enough. He thought despairingly: the child! Up there alone! And without any consideration for his own safety, mindful only that he was the Carrier, he leaped across the threshold, out into the storm.

He sank instantly into deep snow. He scrambled free only to sink again. Clawing at the brittle crust that constantly collapsed beneath him, his body spreadeagled for greater purchase, he somehow floundered his way across to the base of the pinnacle.

The storm was at its height now, the flashes coming so fast that the sky was a blaze of light. Tom had only to glance up to see the creature's stark outline, its fiercely glowing eyes. With its hind legs planted on either edge of the summit, it reared above where the child lay, its head raised triumphantly, tail flicking to and fro in time to the thunder rolls. In its arrogance, it did not once look down to where Tom was slowly clambering skywards. Everything about its attitude bespoke victory. As if with its body alone it was declaring: "See! I have conquered here. This place is mine. I have no challengers."

But what about the child? Tom wondered. Whose sleeping mind contained force enough to resist an avalanche? Was it truly powerless in the face of this creature? Or already trodden underfoot, its tiny limbs strewn bloodily about the summit?

Tom recoiled in horror from the thought of its death, and continued to inch his way upwards, holding on for dear life while the pinnacle shuddered and groaned under the bombardment of the storm.

Even for Tom it was a dangerous climb. Already ugly cracks were appearing in the pinnacle's frozen depths: jagged flaws that mirrored the lightning's zigzag path. Sometimes whole buttressed sections splintered away and threatened to carry him with them. Through it all he pressed on, weathering the shards of ice that rained down, until his fingers curled at last over the lip of the summit.

The creature was standing directly above him. It was far bigger than he had realised, its haunches heavily scaled. And the stench of it! A smell so foul and overpowering that he felt momentarily dizzy. He reached out to steady himself, and his hand closed around one of the spiked talons of the foot. Immediately he was dragged up onto the summit as the creature whirled around towards him.

He looked up into the harsh green of its eyes, into the bloodied deeps of its pupils. They were no longer triumphant. What could he detect there now? Fear perhaps? Loathing? Or mere surprise? Certainly there was something defensive, almost half-hearted, about the way the creature lunged at him. The head drew back, hesitated, and then hacked down short of its mark, the curved beak shattering the ice between his feet. He rolled sideways, into the crystal-encrusted hollow; his hands groped for the back-pack he had so lovingly placed there . . . and encountered nothing! Emptiness!

Where . . .?

He tried to scramble to his feet and was beaten down by a blow from the wings. But now he had seen the pack: over on the far side of the summit, its straps tangled in the creature's talons. Thankfully the flap was closed protectively over the sleeping child, hiding it from view. From a crouched position Tom leaped for the pack, and missed as the creature rose into the air, its wings flapping wildly. He leaped again, reaching high, and managed to catch a dangling loop of strap, his unexpected weight dragging the creature back onto the summit.

As they tumbled together into the hollow, everything seemed to go wrong. The sky tilted and threatened to fall in;

the thunder exploded into a continuous roll; forked lightning laced the air, coming at them from every direction. Tom felt the pinnacle shudder as it was struck again and again. There was a sharp report, louder even than the thunder, and suddenly it was not just the sky that was tilting. The summit was swinging sideways, rocking out of control; and with a shriek of pure rage the creature launched itself into space, drawing Tom and the pack after it.

For a while they were lost in the storm clouds, buffeted by swirls of ice and snow. When they emerged into clearer air, the pinnacle had vanished. Only its fallen outline remained, imprinted on the darkened plain. They were spiralling away from it, the craggy wings spread wide, Tom still holding precariously to the pack with one hand. So as not to further endanger the child, he lunged for and grasped the scaly leg. The moment he did so, the talons jerked apart, as though scalded by his touch, and the pack slipped free and plummeted downwards.

Hanging there, Tom watched with dismay as it dwindled to a speck and disappeared, buried deep in the snow. He knew that no living being could survive such an impact – not himself, nor even the elfin child – yet that did not deter him. Deliberately, he relaxed his grip and let himself fall, determined to share the child's fate.

His body tumbling helplessly, he felt he was drifting rather than falling, the frozen wind moaning past his cheeks. He had forgotten the winged creature. His only thought was for the child. "Wait for me!" he called. "I'm coming!"

He could sense that the snow-covered plain was precariously near, rushing to meet him. He glanced down, noting every detail: the miniature crater where the pack had landed; the thin line of the ridge which marked the edge of the plain. Mentally he readied himself for the sudden shock. For that fleeting moment of blackout. Another second or two and . . . !

There was a beating of wings above his head, a chill touch as spiked talons pierced his clothes and slid across his bare back, and the creature had him again. Instead of falling, he was drawn into a curving dive, skimming so low that his feet scuffed the frosted surface of the ridge. Then he was borne aloft in spite of all his struggles.

"No!" he screamed aloud. "No!" For he understood that this

– to become the captive of the creature – was the worst thing that could happen to him. Worse even than death.

The creature cared nothing for his protest, however. With each surging wingbeat it carried him higher, up through the dwindling storm to where the angry clouds were already parting in readiness.

12 The clouds of pain and fatigue opened onto dim light. His head and chest hurt unbearably. "No," he complained in a weak voice, for hands were reaching down towards him, but nobody would listen. There was a distant shout, and he was hoisted up and jostled roughly.

Some time passed before he realised where he was. He lay draped across Casey's shoulder and was being carried through the winding tunnels of the old workings. Many of the tunnels were half-flooded, the water thrown up by Casey's heels splashing into his face; others had ceilings so low that the roof beams brushed his back and Casey had to stumble along bent almost double. Casey himself was soon gasping for breath and lurching from side to side. Once, when he collided with a timber support, there was a clatter of falling debris behind them, yet still they pressed on, until the background shouts had faded away completely.

Groaning from the prolonged effort, Casey let Tom slide down onto a floor covered with a skim of water. He was glad of its cool touch, the way it soaked through his jacket and shirt, because the atmosphere was stiflingly hot. Airless. Lying there, he believed for a while that the heat and the persistent pain were reasons enough for his feeling of depression. Then he remembered the Dream, and despite his weakness he struggled upright.

"The child!" he burst out miserably. "It's dead!"

The spoked shadows from the lamps reeled and

swung as the others also started to their feet. Three glistening faces ringed him in.

"Dead?" Casey echoed him.

"It can't be!" Angus gasped, his lips almost black in the lamplight.

"There was this . . . this bird-creature," he said, trying to piece together the lingering fragments of the Dream. "It . . . it killed . . ."

Blossom struck him hard across the face. "Never!" she croaked hoarsely, her face twisted in anguish.

"I'm only telling you what I saw," he protested. "This creature, it was like . . . like something out of a nightmare . . ."

"Nightmare!" She leaped upon that one word as if it were their salvation – miming it and nodding her head in approval.

"D'you think that's all it was?" he asked hopefully.

"You've been gassed," Angus explained, his voice light with relief. "Not badly, but enough to affect your dreams. It was the same with me."

"So the child's all right?"

"It lives," Casey said simply. "It always has. You heard what Mr C told us. It's the spirit of the Sleeper, so how can it die?"

Tom nodded, half convinced, the vividness of the Dream already beginning to fade. Like the others, he sank back onto the water-soaked floor, though only for a minute or two. A light flashed at the end of the tunnel, and silently they rose and slunk away, taking care to shield their lamps with their bodies.

As yet, Tom was too weak to run, but with Angus to guide them through the intricate pattern of workings they managed to stay ahead. From galleries waist-deep in water, he led them along side tunnels so low that they had to crawl on hands and knees. At other times they baffled their pursuers by changing levels, squirming up through connecting shafts that were hardly wider than burrows. Each new strategy gained them a small advantage, but never more than that. Always, when they stopped to listen, they could hear the murmur of approaching voices or the squelch and splash of running feet.

In desperation they chose the most dangerous routes they could find: tunnels with timbering so rotten that the roofs sagged and oozed black sludge; or worse, areas deserted even by the rats, where gas, lingering in the fetid air, made them feel heavy-limbed and confused. And still, for all their risks, the sounds of pursuit remained, dogging their weary footsteps.

Soon Tom was barely able to stay upright. Through a fog of nausea and dizziness he blundered on, convinced that each step would be his last. Though in the end it was not he, but Angus who gave up.

Propped wearily against the side wall, his narrow chest heaving, he indicated Tom with one shaky hand. "Carrier . . :" he panted. "Save Carrier . . . not far now . . ."

"Hush your nonsense," Casey said, but was pushed feebly away when he stooped to take Angus's weight.

"No . . . finished," Angus insisted, the hollows in his cheeks almost as dark as the tunnel ahead. "You . . . go on . . ."

"Not unless you come with us," Casey replied.

He shook his head. ". . . stay . . . try and . . . stop hunters . . ."

There was no time for further argument. Lights again appeared in the blackness behind them, bobbing erratically as they were carried swiftly over the uneven ground.

"Tom!" The word echoed through the gloom like the tolling of some distant bell. "Tom!"

"Go . . ." Angus gasped, and before any of them realised what he intended, he was staggering towards the oncoming lights.

Casey tried to follow, but Blossom leaped in his path, her eyes afire from the lamp she thrust out between them.

"Let him go!" she said soundlessly, biting down on the words for emphasis.

Casey hesitated, and already it was too late for any of them to do more than stand there. In silence they heard Angus's footsteps slow to a halt; saw the glowing ball of his lamp swing down to ground level and grow still. After that there was an ominous sound, of wood striking repeatedly against wood.

Chock, chock, chock . . .

"Angus!" Casey bellowed, and suddenly he was wrestling not just with Blossom, but also with Tom – the two of them fighting to hold him, their struggling bodies surrounded by leaping shadows.

In the background the sound of wood against wood continued: *Chock, chock, chock* . . . Followed by a crash as the first of the timber supports fell away.

Something seemed to shift within the hillside – a heavy, sluggish kind of movement, like a giant turning in his sleep – and all at once the advancing lights ceased to bob and weave. Nearer at hand the struggle was over, Tom and his companions now clinging to each other.

Chock, chock, chock . . .

Another support gave way, and the giant stirred more energetically, as if coming slowly awake. He grumbled to himself as he did so, stretching and yawning until the roof groaned in reply.

Chock, chock, chock . . .

Further along the tunnel timbers splintered and snapped, and with a roar the giant was amongst them. The ground shuddered, the distant lights blinked out, and a gust of dank air wafted past Tom's face. Instants later a wave of muddy water slapped against his legs.

"Angus!" Casey called again, shouting the name into the ensuing hush as he jerked free of his companions and lumbered off into the rising tide.

Tom and Blossom came upon him at the point where the tunnel had collapsed. He was crying and tearing at the wall of rock and slime with his bare hands, but as fast as he pulled rocks away, more tumbled down from above. Already the water was nearly up to his waist.

Tom tried pleading with him, but it did no good. He only dug the harder, tears streaming down his cheeks. It was Blossom who made him stop, by striking him with her clenched fist, far harder than she had hit Tom earlier.

Casey turned on her tearfully. "Damn you!" he shouted. "It's your fault he's dead! If you'd let me . . . !"

Tom thought she was about to hit him again, but instead she mouthed two words – "The child" – and as Casey fell silent, she pointed at the dangerously sagging roof. One of the straining boards creaked and let through a spurt of black mud that sprayed their upturned faces.

Casey smeared away the mud almost absent-mindedly. "Yes . . ." he muttered, chastened. "The child." And brushing past them, he waded back along the tunnel.

Their race now was against the steadily rising water. A race they would surely have lost had they not come upon a narrow connecting shaft that led to a higher level. There they rested for a few minutes and plodded on – three bedraggled figures trapped within a soft haze of light, the encroaching darkness crowding in upon them from all sides.

Fatigue proved to be their greatest enemy, for they encountered no further pockets of gas, no floods, no cave-ins. It was simply a question of pressing forward, of not giving in to the fatigue that all but overcame them in the stagnant atmosphere. What helped keep them alert were the many rats inhabiting that part of the mine – sleek-bodied creatures that reared up at their approach, blinded by the light. The constant patter of rats' feet, amplified by the tunnels, often produced eerie effects that made them search the shadows nervously. And once, when a sudden squeak took on the likeness of a voice, Casey spun around, a haunted expression on his face.

"Angus?" he called fearfully. "Is that you?"

But all that peered back at him from the darkness were two beady eyes that flashed silver and red in the lamplight.

Their first indication of a way out came in the form of fresh air. A cool tongue of breeze brushed their cheeks just as they were passing a side tunnel, and they turned and hurried along it. The breeze grew stronger, fresher, became a wind that whistled past them, bringing with it the smell of sun-warmed earth and heather. They broke into a run, lured on by the scent of a world which, secretly, they had thought never to see again: and there, at the end of the tunnel, where the wind seemed to pour magically from a solid wall of rock, was a ladder; and high above, a tiny pin-prick of white light.

The ventilation shaft, which was what they had chanced upon, proved to be much deeper than the shaft they had descended, and the climb back up was both long and tiring. Twice, when Blossom faltered, Tom mounted the ladder alongside her. On each occasion she sank against him almost gratefully; but once recovered, she shrugged him off and climbed on without a word of thanks.

It was mid-afternoon when they reached the surface. Discarding their helmets and lamps, they stood for a while in the full sunlight, glad of its gentle touch. Yet even the soft warmth of the spring day could not disguise the dreariness of the hollow into which they had emerged. A raw gash in the hillside, it looked as if it had been dug during the early years of the mine. Nothing had grown there since. Its sides were discoloured by water oozing from the surface soil, the protruding rocks were covered with slime or sickly-green lichen, and the small lake or pool cupped in the lower reaches was as black as the deeps of the mine itself.

From the rim of this hollow they were able to take their bearings: to discover that they had come out near the very top of the fell. To their relief there was no sign of pursuit, no tell-tale figures labouring up towards them. Their hiding place was surrounded by nothing more threatening than a wind-ruffled sea of heather. The real sea, blue-grey and strangely remote, glinted in the far distance. The town, almost as far off, was reduced to a smudged thumbprint on an otherwise unblemished landscape, its untidy sprawl bounded by the hair-thin line of the cliffs. Only Tower Rock appeared undiminished by the distance, its bulging top, seen from this angle, more than ever like an eyeless mask.

Tom turned his back hastily on the Rock and slid down out of sight. Down towards the pool at the bottom where Blossom was already crouched at the water's edge. She was acting oddly, her eyes closed, head tipped back, nostrils quivering, as if trying to detect something as yet unseen. Some invisible presence perhaps. She seemed to locate it at last because she turned her head sharply, and then nodded and opened her eyes. She was gazing straight at the steepest side of the hollow – the side that never saw the sun – a smile of recognition on her lips.

"What is it?" Tom asked.

"It's here," she answered, mouthing the words carefully so he and Casey would understand. "The child."

"The child? Are you sure?"

She nodded again and pointed to a shelf of rock jutting out over the pool. Its shape alone was enough to stir the hair on the back of Tom's neck, for it was dished like a cradle, its otherwise smooth surface scarred by growths of hard white quartz. Tom closed his eyes as Blossom had done, and suddenly he too was aware of the child's presence. He looked again, and the cradle shape, instead of being empty, was touched with a ghostly shadow or outline. So pale, so delicate, that it shivered and half dissolved in the breeze.

"Is this the place Mr Crawford was talking about?" he asked in an awed whisper. "Where dream and reality are the same?"

She shook her head, but left Casey to answer for her, frowning at him when he hesitated.

"No, we're not there yet," he said, nearly as awe-struck as Tom. "There's a special place we have to get to, where the Dream will come truly alive. That'll be later. According to Mr C, this is just a chance meeting, the kind of thing that can happen sometimes. A ghosting, he calls it."

"A ghosting?" Tom queried. "So the Dream's all around us, is that it?"

Casey shuffled his feet uncomfortably and made no reply; and when Tom turned enquiringly to Blossom, she merely shrugged, as if the question were too difficult, and slipped the bag of food from around her neck – a gesture that served as a sudden reminder of how hungry they all were.

Uneasily, because he could not ignore the ghostly presence sharing the hollow with them, Tom accepted his portion of food and gulped it down. Afterwards, like the others, he quenched his thirst at the pool which had an odd, bitter taste and made him think of a pain-numbing medicine he had been given as a child.

Medicine?

Was he imagining things or did the water bring with it a sense of sleepiness? He tried to stand up, but staggered and fell. There was a leaden feeling in his arms and legs that was more than just fatigue. An unnatural weight that bore him down.

"I have drunk from the cup of Lethe," he muttered aloud – words which meant nothing to him, that had popped into his mind from nowhere, like a gift. They were accompanied by a murmurous chuckle that belonged more to the untroubled surface of the pool, to the lichen-covered rocks, than to himself.

He blinked, striving to bring the hollow into focus. Two vague forms were lying nearby. More ghosts? More fugitives from the Dream? He lifted his eyes to the sun, the shock of its brightness driving sleep away, and saw that the two forms were Blossom and Casey. They lay sprawled out fast asleep on a level section of ground directly beneath the shelf of rock. He could feel their combined wills drawing him in their wake. Their silent voices, twined in song, called temptingly; and as his drug-like weariness returned, he crawled over and lay between them.

Yet still, somehow, he resisted, alert enough to recall what had happened when he had last given way to unwanted sleep. A nightmare – that had been Blossom's word for it. And Angus's too. He let his eyes drift shut, and saw two scaled legs arcing above him; felt the craggy edge of a wing buffet his face. No, he thought in horror, and tried to swim back up through the dark pool, up towards the sunlight. Already it was so far off. And why did he want to reach it anyway? What was there to fear here in the depths? As he struggled for an answer, he heard himself mutter the same unfamiliar words as before:

"I have drunk from the cup of Lethe."

Except that now he understood what the words meant, their meaning proffered to him as another gift. Lethe – the dark stream – that chuckled to itself as it bore him down.

13 He struggled from the clutches of the stream, out into emptiness; into that lightless region that was not really a place at all, but a timeless moment of choice. As always, the choice presented itself as a threshold, an open door, and he crawled towards it and peered through.

The first thing he noticed was the pinnacle – or what was left of it – its shattered sections half buried in the snow. He was not sure why that disturbed him, yet it did, and he drew back slightly, his suspicions aroused. He thought: So the storm actually happened! I didn't just imagine it as they said.

They?

He was vague about that too. And in any case another thought had occurred to him, far more disturbing than the first. If the storm was real, then so was the taloned bird-creature!

Cautiously, standing well back from the threshold, he searched the starless sky, stared keenly into the black space shrouding the horizon, let his eyes move slowly across the shadowy heaps of snow left by the avalanche. No bird-shape showed itself anywhere, no matter how hard he looked. On the other hand he had not located it easily on that previous occasion either. He shuddered at the recollection, determined this time to be more thorough, not to go rushing in as he had before.

Once again he scanned the faintly luminous snow line, examining with renewed care each ridge or dip in its uneven surface. And sure enough, there was a hint of movement! Over to his right, at the very edge of vision!

He swung around, instantly on his guard, but it was only Blossom and Casey, huddled in the shelter of the fallen pinnaolo, thoir palo ooloured olothoo almoot indiotinguichablo from the white background. Apart from being cold – for they were slapping their arms across their chests – they were so obviously at ease in their surroundings that Tom felt re-assured. What was there to fear if they could sit there waiting for him?

He stood up, embarrassed at having delayed for so long, and was about to join them when he noticed something else. Much closer. No more than a pace or two beyond the threshold. A spangled shape lying abandoned in the snow, its polished surface glinting dangerously. He leaned forward for a better view, though he had already guessed what it was. A scale! Identical to those that had covered the haunches of the bird-creature!

In the first moment of recognition, he seemed to hear again the beating of those heavy wings, the scrabble of talons on the icy summit. He ducked and turned instinctively, back towards the emptiness, towards the dark surging stream that had brought him here. Behind him, he heard the door clang shut, his startled cry banishing the Dream before it had truly begun.

14 He came to with a startled cry, all his drowsiness gone. The sun had barely moved, so he knew he could not have been asleep for long. Blossom and Casey were still lying beside him, held by the Dream. He sat up and looked at their sleeping faces which were entirely free of the terror that had driven him back to this dreary hollow. More than ever they reminded him of the child – their eyelids gently quivering, their features touched by a faintly elfin quality that . . .

Elfin?

He scrambled hastily away, wondering for a moment whether he was still asleep. No, the sun shone warm and real on the back of his neck; the breeze carried the heady scent of heather. All the same there was no mistaking the elfin quality in Blossom and Casey's faces, as if the Dream were gradually invading the waking world.

And his own face? Was that also slowly altering? Taking on the lineaments of the child?

He ran down and knelt at the water's edge. Stared at his own reflection locked there in the blackness. Because of the ripples on the pool's surface, it was difficult to be certain, but yes . . . there did appear to be some change. To the eyes especially. And was it just the effect of the sun behind him, or did his hair form a golden fringe about his head? He took a handful of it and yanked hard. Although the tuft that came away was mainly dark, it was interlaced with bright yellow threads!

He did not panic, or feel elated either. Squatting in the mud at the pool's verge, he tried to work out what it all meant. Why, for instance, did he feel disturbed about becoming like the child? Wasn't it natural for him, as Carrier, to be affected by his task? Even the mill- and mine-workers, bonded by the sameness of their labour, came to have a recognisable look about them. So why should he be any different? Also, hadn't Mr Crawford warned him that he would eventually reach a place where Dream and reality merged? Perhaps this present change was a part of that merging process. Unless, of course, it was the result of the child's ghostly presence in the hollow.

He glanced up at the shelf of rock, seeking there for the truth. At first the rock seemed empty, but then he remembered something his father had taught him: how, to see the fainter stars in the night sky, it is better to look just to one side of them. He did much the same now, shifting his gaze a little to the left of the rock, and straight away he saw it: the shadowy silhouette of a head, of an outflung arm and hand.

"What are you doing here?" he murmured, softly challenging the child's half-seen shade. "Why aren't you waiting for me in the Dream? Or . . ." He waved one hand vaguely at the surrounding hollow. ". . . or is the Dream hidden here somewhere? Behind all this?"

He waited expectantly, but the ghostly outline did not stir; and it came to Tom that he had asked a similar question of Blossom earlier, and been ignored by her too. Well, he wouldn't be ignored any longer. Suddenly he was quite definite about that. As the Carrier – as someone who had been driven from his home and family – he had the right to understand what was going on. If no one would explain it all to him, then he would find out for himself, never mind that he still felt weak and unwell from his experience in the mine.

Edging past his sleeping companions, he clambered out of the hollow. Still nobody was to be seen anywhere on the open fell, though only a short distance above him it ended in a kind of crest or ridge which masked what lay beyond. He approached this crest warily, crawling the last few metres and carefully parting the heather to peer through to the other side.

What he saw made him start to his feet. Beneath him lay a huge expanse of open country, as flat as any plain except that it was tilted slightly downwards. He closed his eyes, to steady himself, but when he looked again, there it was still, as utterly familiar as before. The landscape of the Dream! None other! True, it now wore a mantle of heather rather than snow, but that was a small difference. The lie of the land was identical, with every detail exactly in place. This very ridge on which he stood had clipped his heels when the bird-creature had carried him skimming across the plain; there, some way down the slope, was the roughened area of the avalanche; much further off he could just discern the band of ridged and broken country where he had fled through the mist; and further away still, all but lost in the haze, gleamed the cliffs from which he had first set out.

As in a sunlit version of the Dream, he walked on, threading a path through the heather. By the time he reached the spot where the avalanche had thundered down, the sun had dipped much lower and a chill had crept into the day. In the tired yellow light of late afternoon he contemplated the remains of the pinnacle—shattered sections of ancient black rock half buried in the grey soil. It did not come as a surprise that he should find it there. Nor was he surprised by the two pallid ghosts, shot through by sunlight, that huddled beside a blunt-ended length of rock. These, too, he had anticipated.

"Blossom?" he called. "Casey?"

There was an answering cry, high and clear, but it came only from a formation of birds winging their way home in the last of the golden light. The two transparent forms did not once look up and acknowledge him, not even when he reached out to touch them, his hand encountering nothing but thin air and the weathered surface of the rock under which they sheltered.

He turned away, disappointed, intent on finding the

threshold he had not dared to cross. Where it had been, there was now a furrow of bare earth. He placed one foot upon it, and the whole evening seemed to grow fuzzy and indistinct, almost ghostly. He shook his head, and instantly everything was back to normal. The ground was again streaked with sharp bands of shadow, the sun sinking slowly beneath the horizon. Just before it disappeared, something caught his eye, over to the left: a flash and dazzle of reflected light.

His heart lurched uncomfortably as he stooped and pulled aside an obscuring strand of heather. Beneath it lay a slab of flint blacker than the pool in the hollow; and set into its surface, a familiar spangled shape!

For some seconds he could not move. He could hardly breathe. Even when his heart steadied he stayed crouching there, unable to deny what he had found. Not just the scale, but its fossilised remains. Fossilised! Unbelievably ancient. Older than the whole of human existence!

But how was that possible when he had been carried by the creature only hours earlier? When he had seen the scaled and living haunches with his own eyes?

Tentatively, he reached out to touch it, and the sun slid from view, plunging the world into twilight. He shivered as the full chill of the evening descended. Raising his head, he looked furtively out across the rapidly darkening plain. Instinct warned him that this was no place to be alone; while another, more thoughtful, part of himself made him linger on.

Here at his feet was a fragment of the Dream. Physical proof that events in the Dream and events in the present somehow coincided. The scale was a kind of link between the two. Possessing it would be like possessing the Dream itself; like holding it in his hand in the here and now; perhaps even having power over it.

Power? Over the bird-creature? That one idea kept him rooted to the spot, despite the gathering shades of night; despite the pulse of wingbeats high overhead – which he knew to be birds hurrying homewards through the dusk, but which made him shiver just the same. Again he looked up, at the slowly emerging stars, finding in their twinkling light a certain reassurance. And on impulse he took his clasp-knife from his pocket and opened the main blade. Working by feel alone, for he could see almost nothing at ground level, he located the raised area of the scale and slipped the blade beneath its edge. There was a slight resistance, and then a faint crack as it broke away in one piece. He had it! A small, roughly triangular shape that sat like a sliver of ice in the centre of his palm. So cold that it seemed to carry within itself all the wintry quality of the frozen land from which it had come.

He pocketed it hastily and stood up. The plain was lost in obscurity, the stars were as yet too faint to cast any real light. All he could make out was the crest which marked the top of the fell, and he stumbled towards it, constantly tripping over as the heather tangled about his knees and ankles. Tired and sick after his ordeal in the mine, he was often tempted not to get up; to close his eyes there and then and remain enveloped in the heather's soft fragrance. What urged him to his feet, always, was the thought of where he was: still in the vicinity of the pinnacle, the place where the bird-creature had first made its appearance. He had only to imagine his sleeping body lying helpless beneath those glaring green eyes, those spiked talons, and immediately he found the strength to blunder on.

Once beyond the crest he felt safer, lulled by the homely smell of the sea now being borne to him on the night wind. So that when he tripped over yet again, he could see no good reason why he should not stay where he was. For a while anyway. He sank down, meaning to doze for just a few minutes, but the speed of his descent caught him unprepared, and in one swift step he had moved from darkness to darkness.

15 The portal appeared so suddenly that he was unprepared for it. One step and he was through, the intense cold closing on him like a vice. He pulled his wool-lined collar up around his chin and glanced warily down, his eyes automatically searching for the fallen scale. Where it had lain, there was now only bare snow. No, on closer inspection he saw it was not quite bare: the crusted surface bore the imprint of a shallow triangular shape, as if someone . . . as if something had been . . . But as always it was like trying to remember the details of another life, of another person, and he soon gave up. All that really concerned him was the absence of the bird-creature. For the time being, every vestige of its existence had disappeared, leaving the day calm and grey, empty of any obvious threat.

He was distracted by a high chirrup of unheard song. Casey and Blossom had abandoned the shelter of the shattered pinnacle and were wading through the snow towards him. They looked more puzzled than worried. There was also more than a hint of impatience in the way Blossom tossed back her head in challenge, her mouth opening onto a single word:

"Where?"

The answer came readily to him, two memories locking together in his mind. One was of his own pack plummeting down to leave a miniature crater in the snow; the other was of a murmurous chuckle, oddly close and confidential, which had indicated that all was well. And without hesitation he turned and made for the low crest that marked the edge of the plain, leaving Casey and Blossom to trudge along behind.

On the far side of the crest the land fell steeply away: a long snow-covered slope that plunged down and down towards some kind of primitive settlement. Even seen from a distance, with the icy wind stinging their eyes, it was not an enticing place, hardly more than a scatter of hovels that showed as a dirty grey stain on the snow. It was dominated by an imposing tower made entirely of ice which seemed to gather to itself all the light in the overcast day. Its polished sides sparkled brilliantly; its bulging top was festooned with what appeared to be gleaming threads. Beyond the magnificence of the tower the wasteland continued: a flat white expanse much vaster and no less dreary than anything Tom had encountered so far, which stretched on and out towards the great circle of the horizon.

Was that where they were making for, Tom wondered, out there? Where land and sky vied with each other in monotony? Where life, movement, colour, had no place? He recoiled from the idea, his eyes drawn back to the tower. Compared with the settlement and the distant plain, it was like a vision of beauty; a sanctuary in the midst of so much dullness; a glittering spike of frosty light that had powered itself clear of its sordid surroundings. The loveliness of it filled him with longing. Undeterred by its height, by its sheer sides, he found himself hoping that here at last was their true destination, the child's ultimate resting place. With a sense of secret delight, he imagined the long and hazardous climb upwards; that final moment when he would . . .

But Blossom, her impatience again getting the better of her, was prodding him in the back, and he wrenched his eyes from the tower and led the way down the slope, moving crab-wise through the deep snow to keep his balance.

He had not gone far when he detected a presence in the immediate vicinity. A sleeping figure, glimpsed from the corner of his eye, which disappeared as soon as he turned to look. He stopped and the others blundered into him, their bewilderment expressed in a trill of high song. He answered by pointing to the vague imprint of a body in the snow, a ghostly outline which moved restlessly even as he watched. Its back was towards him, its face hidden. He was glad of that, unwilling as yet to acknowledge the identity of this silent sleeper; relieved when the others patted him reassuringly and urged him on, down to where the crater opened suddenly at their feet.

There were ghostly sleepers here as well. Two of them lying side by side near a pool of black ice. They were less of a surprise than the crater itself. Seen from above, on that stormy night, it had looked small, exactly the size of hole the pack would have punched into the snow; whereas this was large, a great scoop gouged from the hillside, as if the bird-creature, in its eagerness to reach the child, had struck at the snow again and again. It amazed Tom that the child had survived such an ordeal unscathed; that it should be lying here so peacefully, couched on a jewel-encrusted ledge that jutted out over the pool.

At Blossom's bidding, he clambered down to the ledge. As ever, the child had suffered no ill-effects from the cold. The exposed skin of its face and neck glowed a warm pink; the veins in the wrist of its outflung arm throbbed gently; the perfectly curved lashes retained a moist, dewy quality that spoke more of spring than of winter. While Tom hovered above its sleeping face, the eyelids quivered as though about to open, and he waited expectantly for those soft grey eyes to gaze up at him. But only the lips parted, in a contented sigh, the childish breath so sweet and fresh that Tom forgot his disappointment, forgot the raw nature of the day. With a renewed sense of purpose, he swung the pack up onto his shoulders, gratified by the way the child moulded its tiny body to his.

Casey and Blossom were waiting on the lower lip of the crater. Now that he had resumed his task as Carrier, they responded differently to him. Casey's protectiveness was mingled with respect; and some of Blossom's old resentment had returned. When he tried to walk alongside her, she brushed him away and moved sullenly on ahead, forcing her crippled body through the deepening drifts.

Seen against the vastness of the landscape, she looked particularly vulnerable, and he yearned to call her back, unhappy that there should be any jealousy between them. Floundering along in her wake, he considered how best to win her over. There was, he realised, one sure way: to let her carry the child for a while; for them both to share the burden. That would appease her, and no possible harm would come to the child – he was sure of that.

The child, however, seemed to guess his purpose because it began to squirm uncomfortably, its body rigid with refusal; and simultaneously an unknown voice whispered to him.

"Not yet."

He spun around, searching the surrounding slope. Apart from Casey, whose mouth and nose were muffled against the cold, no one else was close by. No secret companion had stolen up on them. Tom turned back towards Blossom and reached tentatively for his shoulder straps . . . and the voice was there again, whispering the same message as before. "Not yet." In the same quiet tone of authority. Though now there was no doubting where it came from – somewhere within his own mind.

Shaken, he stumbled and had to spread his arms winglike on the snow to prevent himself falling. As much as the voice itself, it was the suggestiveness of the message that unsettled him. Not yet? What was it supposed to mean? That he was the Carrier only for the present? That in time he would be asked to give the child up? He probed deeper, trying to search the voice out, to discover its source, and encountered only an icy wall of silence which he could not break through.

None the less the implied threat of the whispered message remained. Stung by it, he was about to slip the pack from his shoulders when he noticed that Blossom was walking erratically, weaving drunkenly from side to side.

"Blossom!" he cried, and the boom of his voice made the earth and sky shrink in upon themselves, the clouds dip lower.

She responded by breaking into a stumbling run, fleeing from him, her hands stretched out blindly.

Casey was the first to reach her. Bounding across the trampled snow, he encircled her with both arms. She tried to avoid his gaze, but he jerked her face up towards him. And Tom, peering over Casey's shoulder, saw the reason for her distress: the whites of both eyes, formerly so clear, had grown discoloured and were flecked with red.

"She's snow-blind," he said quietly.

She nodded, and as Casey released her she crumpled to

her knees. For once she had no need of speech. Her bitter expression, the dejected slump of her shoulders, told their own story.

Casey crouched beside her and grasped her hands in his, his high song never more delicate and tender. Like frosted gossamer drifting through the brittle air, it spoke of things Tom only half understood. Of their continuing need of her. Of how she had vowed to stay with the Carrier, to accompany him to the very end, just to be sure.

Tom would have liked to know what they were so unsure of. Was he, Tom, the cause of their anxiety? Did they not trust him? Perhaps. But then this was not the time for such questions. The one pressing issue was Blossom's present condition.

Taking off his scarf, he tested it first on himself, by stretching it across his eyes. Because it was loosely woven, it kept out most of the glare while allowing through just enough light for him to see a dim outline of things.

"Here," he murmured, and wound the scarf about her head as a blindfold.

She did not resist. She even leaned her head forward so he could tie a knot at the back of her neck. She would not let him help her up, though. Her mouth drawn into a thin line of resignation, she rejected his proffered hand and reached out instead to Casey. Similarly it was Casey whom she chose as a guide when they resumed their journey down the slope. So that Tom, walking on ahead through the fresh snow, was made to wonder anew why she refused to trust or rely on him.

More determined than ever to win that trust, he kept a sharp lookout, uneasily aware of the hunters' long absence. Every few paces he scanned the hillside, searching for any revealing specks of black. Yet for all his vigilance, it was Blossom in the end who sounded the warning, her blindness serving only to heighten her other senses. There was a faint tremor of song from behind him, and he turned to find her standing quite still, her head raised and alert, one mittened hand pressed to her lips. He also listened, straining to hear past the moan of the wind. In the brief lulls there was hardly a sound – just the harmless twitter of a bird.

A bird? In this wasteland? This emptiness?

Casey had grown suspicious too. Stepping in front of Blossom, he drew a cudgel from his pack.

120

Still there was nothing to be seen but a nearby tumble of boulders. One of them moved, as if dislodged by the wind. Uncoiled itself and stood upright. Snow cascading from its shoulders, the black clothes and pale face showing through. A face which once again Tom recognised; which he knew almost as well as his own. The most familiar face of them all, and the most dreaded, with jutting jaw and piercing blue eyes.

It was the eyes which suggested the name to him. As cold and hard as . . . Steele! Jack!

"You'll never wake the Sleeper!" Jack bellowed, and the frozen hillside buckled under the impact of his words, the sky trembled and tore loose from the horizon, allowing warm darkness to come flooding through.

Tom very nearly let the darkness take him, pluck him free of all danger. Then he remembered the child – how it would be left exposed here on the hillside – and he clutched at the straps of his pack and willed the sky to grow steady; willed the dark gash in the horizon to close.

Already Jack was upon him. Surprisingly, there was no anger in his face. Only cold determination. Tom could not move, mesmerised by the man's unfeeling stare, by the cudgel's downward swing. At the last moment he threw up his hands defensively, but Casey had already leaped in Jack's path, the cudgel felling him instead of Tom. Somehow Casey struggled up and even managed to return the blow, he and Jack crashing together and rolling off down the slope.

Other hunters had shrugged off their snowy camouflage and were closing in. But the child, which had lain so still during Jack's attack, was also stirring: sighing in a way Tom had never heard before, its long snoring breaths matching the uneven pulse of the wind which rose in force and rose again. At the third or fourth blast, Tom could barely keep his feet. The gale was coming at him from every direction, flinging up waves of snow that cut visibility to a few paces. He just had time to reach Blossom's side before the surrounding world disappeared in a complete white-out.

Without a muffler to protect his face, Tom was as blind as Blossom, and as helpless. Heads down, arms linked so as not to be separated, they reeled under the mounting force of the

storm. Like sheep, they were driven by it this way and that –
first up the slope, then down, then straight across, in an
irregular pattern impossible to predict – while behind them
the wind and snow together scoured away their footprints.

Eventually, exhausted by the constant buffeting, they sank
down in the lee of an icy boulder. There they clung to each
other for what felt like hours, preserving the remaining heat
in their bodies as the wind shrieked and moaned in fury.

When at last the storm died down, it did so as suddenly as
it had risen. There was a final ferocious gust of wind, and
after that perfect stillness. Silence. The air thick with snow
that settled soundlessly all around them.

Blossom was stiff with cold by the time the air cleared. Tom,
warmed by the closeness of the child, helped her to her feet
and dusted the brittle-dry snow from their heads and
shoulders. As usual, she barely acknowledged him, her head
turned blindly to the tower which soared upwards from the
edge of the plain. In the steadily greying light it seemed almost
to shine out, like a beacon summoning them forward.

Taking her hand, he tried to lead her towards it, but she
held back, hesitant.

"Casey?" she asked, the name mouthed with strangely loving care, her face never turning from the distant tower.

"I don't know," he confessed. "He was still fighting when
the storm came."

"With him?" Again she made no sound, and yet the force
behind that one word was unmistakable.

"Yes, with him," he said, and felt a deep tremor pass
through her.

He gave her a few minutes to collect herself, the blindfold
twitching as she fought to control her feelings. Then, hand in
hand, they moved off, making directly for what Tom now
accepted as their one true destination.

Because the snow had not yet packed down, they made slow
progress. At every step they sank to their thighs and sometimes
almost to their waists. Soon their lower garments were
sodden, their legs aching with cold, so they were glad when
the light began to wane, even though the tower seemed hardly
any nearer.

While there was still enough daylight to see by, Tom paused

and looked around, searching the barren hillside for some place of safety – for that hidden sanctuary which always appeared when they needed it most. He had a clear idea of it in his mind: a glittering cave or grotto carefully fashioned to receive the child. That was why the sight of the two dwellings came as a shock. In this land empty even of birds, they looked oddly out of character, like images lingering in the memory from some other time and place. Blackened and grimy, they stood out sharply against the surrounding whiteness: two dingy hovels, low and windowless, each with a dirty wisp of smoke rising from its roof.

The door of the nearer one opened and a woman emerged, her tangled hair tied in a knot at the nape of her neck, her skinny body bent almost double and clothed in nothing but rags. Seeing strangers, she gave a yelp of fear and bolted back inside, slamming the door behind her.

Tom would have preferred to keep his distance. Especially when he noticed the figurine set above the doorway: a wood-carving of a taloned, beaked creature with scaled haunches and lion-like tail.

"Not there!" he murmured, and despite the thickening dusk and the rapidly plunging temperature, he would have hurried on had Blossom not clutched him by the arm.

"You don't know what it's like!" he whispered fiercely. "It's not fit to . . ."

He broke off as she tore away her blindfold and pointed at the darkening sky. "Now!" she announced silently, the very urgency with which she mouthed the word reminding him of what he should have realised already. Not just that it was late, but that this was the place they had been brought to. This and no other. And therefore this was where they had to stay, regardless of how unlikely it might look.

Grudgingly, he accompanied her to the first of the hovels and knocked on the wooden lintel. There was no answer. Only the sound of something heavy being dragged across the door-way.

At her insistence they approached the second, slightly smaller dwelling which was decorated with a similar carving. Here the doorway was closed off only by a tattered piece of leather. It flapped aside as they stepped through, into a dim, foul smelling interior. A fire smouldered in the middle of the stamped-earth floor, its smoke drifting up to a hole in the roof. Two ragged figures crouched before the fire. They turned as Tom and Blossom entered, a look of alarm on their malnourished faces. Scurrying forward, they knelt at Tom's feet and touched their foreheads to the ground, muttering all the while in a language he had never heard before. Low and guttural, it sounded so foreign to his ears that he could not even identify their tone of voice. Fear or reverence? He could not be sure.

When he failed to respond, they took a blackened cooking pot from the fire and offered it to him. The smell of the food wafted up and caught in the back of his throat, making him cough and push the pot away. The smell was not unpleasant in itself, but like their language, like the very idea of hunger, he found it completely foreign.

It occurred to him then that since entering this wasteland he had felt neither hunger nor thirst. He had more or less assumed that such sensations did not belong here. These two starved faces, staring beseechingly at him, told him how wrong he was. For them, hunger was an ever-present reality.

There were other surprises in store now that his eyes had grown accustomed to the gloom. A row of half-cured hare skins dangled from the rafters, a flint-bladed knife and axe hanging beside them. A real live hawk, its head hooded, clung to a perch that jutted from a supporting roof-pole. Off to one side, and equally alive, were the gaunt shapes of several moon-eyed cattle, their homely smell adding to the rank odour of the room. And most disturbing of all, in the far corner stood a stone effigy of the bird-creature, with beads of green glass for eyes. It was set on a kind of altar, and a tallow candle burned before it.

Tom turned questioningly to Blossom, but for once she showed little of her usual confidence. Eyes closed, her head thrown back, she was like an animal scenting the breeze, her nostrils flared as she breathed in the mixed odours, all of them so unexpectedly lifelike, so real.

"Look," he said, and steered her towards the effigy in the corner.

But even the soft candlelight was too much for her, and he

124

had to take off her mittens and let her touch the creature. She traced its outline slowly, carefully, her hands, and then her lips beginning to tremble as she moved from talons to scaled haunches and up to the craggy pinions of its wings. When she reached the cruelly-hooked beak, she snatched her hands away and groped clumsily for Tom's pack where the child slept on.

Its calm breaths seemed to steady her, because she turned back quickly and snuffed out the candle. Behind her the two owners of the hut threw themselves to the ground, babbling unintelligibly, but she ignored them. Squinting into the gloom, for which her damaged sight was better suited, she searched the darkening interior. She was interrupted briefly by a warning flash of light, like an eye fluttering open upon day. Then, as the dusk settled back and deepened, she pointed to a much lower doorway set into the end wall.

She and Tom ducked through, into a freezing chamber cut from the snow that lay banked against the side of the dwelling. It must originally have been intended as a storeroom because a few scraggy carcasses of hares still littered the floor, but more recently it had been adapted for another use altogether. Its rough-hewn walls, which gave off a greenish glow, were embossed with glittering nobs of ice; crystal slivers of icicle, twisted and entwined, speared down from the low ceiling; and most important of all, the floor sloped inwards to form a cradle-shaped hollow.

Blossom let out a sobbing sigh of relief and plucked impatiently at Tom's sleeve. Again there was a brilliant flash, a single blink of light, soon gone, which left them in a darkness softened by the faint green glow. Hurriedly, Tom slipped the pack free and lowered the child to the floor. It curled readily into the prepared hollow, untroubled by the bloodied carcasses that lay within reach of its outflung arm, or by the twisted daggers of ice that hovered above. The very peacefulness of its elfin face declared that nothing here could disturb it; that this unlikely chamber, too, was a place of safety.

Was that really so? Tom experienced a sudden chill of doubt as something blundered noisily into the dwelling behind them. He and Blossom ducked back inside, almost colliding with the two ragged owners who were scampering away to hide amongst the cattle. The cause of their fear, looming in the open doorway, was a tall figure. So tall that when it started forward, it cracked its head on a roof-beam and sprawled full-length in the dirt beside the fire. By the dim light of the glowing coals, Tom saw its face, a livid bruise running from the temple down past the mouth to the point of the jaw.

"Casey!" he cried, and would have run to him had the light not flashed for the third and last time.

16 "Casey!" he cried, and opened his eyes onto a sunlit morning.

He looked around expectantly, but found he was alone, lying on a bed of living heather, with the early mist lifting from the surrounding fell. Rising groggily, his head filled with a jumble of dark and conflicting images, he made his way down to the hollow where Casey and Blossom were seated beside the pool, having only just woken. Casey, he could not help noticing, had a vague discoloration on one side of his face, more the ghost of a bruise than an actual mark; and Blossom, although her eyes were clear, was squinting slightly and shielding her face from the sun.

Up until then the Dream had been fading rapidly from his mind, but seeing his two companions like this – still drugged with sleep, still entangled in that other grey world – brought back to him the disturbing events of the night. And they in turn reminded him of another event, equally disturbing: the real-life discovery he had made on the previous evening. Quickly, he thrust a hand into his pocket, to check that his imagination wasn't playing tricks on him. No, the scale was still there, ice-cold against his palm. As actual and undeniable as the squalid hovels in the Dream, or as the upper portion of Tower Rock which was already showing through the mist.

He squatted down beside Blossom, the scale clutched in his hand to give him confidence. "The Dream isn't just going on inside our heads, is it?" he said, challenging rather than questioning her "It's all happening right here, on these hillsides. Isn't that so?"

She shrugged, feigning sleepy indifference.

"And that's not all," he plunged on. "When we enter the Dream, we don't become part of some imaginary time, do we? We step back into the ancient past. Into history."

She glanced sharply at him, suddenly wide awake, and shook her head.

"Yes," he countered, and was about to show her the scale when a sudden sense of caution made him hesitate. The scale, after all, related to a part of the Dream she had not experienced. Better, he decided, to stick to those experiences they had shared. "You saw those huts and the people inside them," he went on. "They were straight out of the Stone Age. Those people hadn't even discovered metal. They were using knives and axes made of flint."

Again she shook her head, her eyes bright with antagonism. "Not the past!" she said, mouthing the words emphatically.

"Why not? It looked real enough to me, and people would only have lived that way long ago."

One hand to her throat, she turned imploringly to Casey, begging him to speak for her.

His gaze, as his eyes met Tom's, was entirely free of doubt. "Long ago is long ago," he said simply, "and the Dream's the Dream. That makes them different in my book."

"You still haven't told me why."

"Because I've listened to what Mr C has to say," he answered with the same easy confidence. "He's told us all about the past. Lots of times. How it was a time of happiness and freedom. Not like today. Not like it is in the Dream either."

"But what if Mr Crawford's wrong?" Tom suggested, picturing again the half-starved faces, the filth and squalor of the hovels. "What if the past wasn't a golden time after all? What if the Dream's just shown us the past as it truly was? As ugly and horrible?"

"I can't agree with that," Casey insisted. "If you ask

128

me, the Dream's the Dream and nothing else. It's not meant to be good or happy. How could it be? It's where they banished him, remember."

"Him?"

"The child, the spirit of the Sleeper," Casey answered promptly, and was supported by a vigorous nod from Blossom.

Tom stood up, undecided, still mindful of the cold touch of the scale against his palm; of the fact that he had prised it from a flint which stretched backwards in time to an incredibly ancient period. In which case surely Mr Crawford *had* to be mistaken. Stepping into the Dream *had* to be like stepping back into the past. A time of poverty and fear, of . . . But then how could the Sleeper be wise and loving? Someone the present world needed? Surely if he was a part of all that horror, he too had to be . . . Had to be what? As ugly as the twin hovels? As cruel and inhuman as the bird-creature? If so, there remained the problem of why people like Mr Crawford and Blossom believed in him. Were they all deluded, and he, Tom, somehow right?

Tom drew in his breath, baffled. It all seemed too difficult. Also, he was troubled by the idea that he was right and everyone else wrong. For the time being at least, it was easier to go along with what the others believed, despite his doubts.

"So the Dream's just a version of all this," he said in a resigned voice, and waved his hand vaguely at the surrounding hollow. "A more horrible version, worse than the mine or the mill or anything in the town."

"That's about it, Tom," Casey affirmed. "It's why we can't leave the child there. We have to get it out, whatever the cost."

Whatever the cost! Within the Dream he had understood the cost instinctively. One glimpse of that icy tower, splendid in its isolation, had convinced him of what lay ahead. Its glittering beauty had drawn him on, made him look forward to the final challenge of the climb. Whereas here, in the sunlit world, its rocky counterpart filled him with dread – a dread he had hoped to leave behind when Jack had driven him from the cliffs. Yet had he really left it behind? Or as in the Dream, was his escape from Jack merely bringing him full circle, back to where he had begun?

"The . . . the place where the Sleeper's hidden . . ." he asked uncertainly, ". . . where the two worlds meet . . . is it . . . ?" He paused, finding it hard to go on, as fearful of the answer as he was of the Rock itself. "I mean . . . is that why you needed me? Because I'm a climber? Because only a climber could hope to reach . . . to reach . . . ?"

They were both watching him, saying nothing.

"Tell me," he pleaded.

Casey glanced away, embarrassed, but Blossom went on staring at him, her manner cool and appraising, with no hint of pity.

"We all have to pay a price, Tom," Casey said gently. "Think of Angus and Bonny and all the rest. You can't pay a higher price than they have. None of us can. Like Mr C says, the golden times aren't to be had for free. We have to win them from the likes of Jack."

"I know," he said, "but I'm not just being asked to fight, like the others, am I? I'm expected to climb the . . . to climb . . ." Again he could not continue, could not speak aloud the thing he dreaded most.

"Think of the child," Casey added, his voice dropping lower. "How can he reach the Sleeper without a climber like you? That's what being the Carrier means. It's for you to get him up there. Blossom and me, we're only here to help, though we'll stay with you for as long as we can, Tom. For as long as we're spared. You know that, don't you?"

He nodded, convinced of their loyalty. Convinced also that somehow, somewhere, he had passed the point where he could abandon the child and turn back. His only road, now, lay forward. But to what? To Tower Rock? Yes, in the depths of his heart he knew the Rock to be his one true destination – here in the waking realm as well as in the Dream. Tower Rock. Where the Dream and the real world were destined to meet. Where the Sleeper himself lay waiting, impatient for Tom's arrival.

Miserably, he hunched down between his companions while Blossom shared out a little more of the food. Because they did not dare drink from the pool a second time, it proved to be a dry tasteless meal, soon over. Then they were on their way again, treading in the footsteps of their own ghostly selves.

Except that now, in the sunlight, it was not the icy spire, but the gloomy shape of Tower Rock that beckoned them on. Whenever Tom looked up, there it was, dark against the sparkling blue of the sea. A hateful sight that reminded him anew of what the future held for him. And rather than travel constantly with his fear, he kept his eyes lowered, busying himself in a search for other recognisable landmarks from the Dream.

There was only one he was sure of. A scatter of boulders some distance down the slope, where Jack had ambushed them. It was unlikely that Jack would try that again. Not there, anyway. Unless of course . . .

Tom stopped and crouched low in the heather. "Those boulders," he hissed. "We'd better give them a wide berth."

"No need for that," Casey answered cheerfully, waving him on. "Jack's too much of a fox to use the same place twice."

"Maybe that's what he expects us to think," Tom said.

It was a warning Blossom at least took seriously. Drawing Casey down beside her, she indicated that they should skirt the whole area by working further across the slope. They agreed silently, and scurried away along the narrow gaps between the heather.

They were not the only watchful ones on the hillside, however, and they had not gone far when the first halloo rang out and a series of dark figures rose up from amongst the boulders.

For once Tom and his companions had a good start. They made the most of it by bounding straight across the top of the heather, using the dense carpet of growth as a kind of springboard to launch themselves downhill at hectic speed. Even so, with Casey's lameness and Blossom's lack of stamina to hamper them, they gradually lost ground to the fastest of the hunters. Moreover, in such open country there was nowhere for them to hide. From the upper ridge all the way down to the distant cliffs, the clean sweep of the fell was interrupted only twice, by the parallel slashes of road and railway line.

Blossom's fall was what decided them. Misjudging the gap between bushes, she crashed down through the heather and winded herself too badly to go on. Although the others helped her as far as the road, clearly the race was lost.

"I say we stand and fight," Casey announced grimly, and began hunting along the dusty verge for some form of weapon.

Before he could find anything, there was a dull rumble, and a gleaming new motor car came rattling down the road towards them, lurching and swaying on the rutted surface. Tom did not pause to consider his next move. Leaping out into the road, he waved his arms wildly, and the car slithered to a halt in a cloud of dust.

The driver, an elderly man wearing cap and goggles and black leather gauntlets, peered around the windscreen at him. "What's this?" he laughed. "Highway robbery?"

Tom blurted out the first thing that came into his head. "My friend's been hurt," he said, pointing to Blossom who was crouched breathlessly by the roadside.

"You'll be miners then?" the man asked in a more serious voice, eyeing their grimy clothes and faces.

"Aye, miners," Tom agreed quickly, conscious all the time of Jack and his followers rapidly approaching across the open fell. "There was a cave-in, and we brought her out through an old shaft just up the hill. We need to get her to a doctor."

The man scratched his chin thoughtfully. "Well, I'll be passing through Seaforth," he said, naming a fishing village further down the coast. "As I recall, there's a doctor there, and you're more than welcome to a ride."

"We're much obliged to you," Tom said, and hurried to help Blossom over to the car.

"But Seaforth's in the wrong direction," Casey objected softly, sidling up beside him.

"If we don't get out of here now," Tom whispered back, "we won't be going anywhere at all."

Casey nodded reluctantly, and between them they lifted Blossom onto the rear seat and climbed in after her.

By then the hallooing of the hunters was so loud and urgent that it sounded clear above the throb of the motor. Jack himself was nearest of all, straining to reach them.

"Friends of yours?" the driver asked, easing the car into motion.

"Workmates," Tom replied, trying to sound relaxed even though he was gripping the edge of the seat with both hands. "That's their way of wishing us well."

"Aah, it's good to see a bit of caring amongst people," the man said, and with a cheery wave he opened the throttle, so that Jack, who had just leaped down onto the road, was lost in fresh coils of dust.

Tom leaned back with a sigh, feeling safer than he had all morning. Not only because he had evaded Jack, but also because of Tower Rock which lay behind them at last, growing further and further away with each lurch of the car.

"So is this your first time in one of these new-fangled devices?" the driver asked, shouting above the road noise.

"Aye, and I hope it's our last," Casey answered with unexpected force.

The man glanced around, surprised, his goggles making him look oddly inhuman. "Why's that, young fellow?"

"There's too many machines in this world already," Casey said bluntly. "I can't see that they do anyone much good. We'd be better off without the lot of them."

The man pursed his lips, considering the idea. "You may be right," he said at last. "Mechanical things can be more trouble than they're worth, even a beauty like this. One minute they're our servants, the next our masters. But I'll tell you what. There's no going back to the days of horses and such like. That's just a dream, and a bad one in the bargain. Human beings aren't meant to be forever looking backwards. For us, the road to the future is as real as this road we're riding on now." He laughed. "And a deal smoother, I hope. Though smooth or bumpy, we can't choose but follow it."

Casey showed every sign of wanting to argue further, but Blossom shook her head and he fell into a sullen silence.

Because of the constant dust and noise, which made conversation difficult, little more was said for the rest of the trip. For his part Tom was amazed that Blossom did not insist on stopping the car once they were well away from Jack. Instead, she settled into her seat, a pensive look in her eyes, apparently content to let the car carry them beyond the fell and the hard line of the cliffs, into softer rolling countryside, and finally down towards the much gentler shore where Seaforth was situated.

They were dropped outside the doctor's surgery in the cobbled main street, the man driving off with another of his cheery waves. Here, where there was no mill or mine, their grubby appearance attracted immediate attention, and they quickly made their way back up the street and out into open country.

"So what now?" Tom asked.

They were trudging along a narrow lane bordered on both sides by high banks.

"It beats me why we came this far in the first place," Casey grumbled. "The only way back is by train, and Jack's sure to be on the watch for us."

"Then why not hide out around here?" Tom suggested.

Casey gave him a resentful, untrusting look. "What good'll the Dream be then? Unless we meet up with it, it'll stay just what it is – a Dream and nothing more."

Tom's hand stole furtively to the icy-cold scale in his pocket. "I think it's always been more than that," he said uneasily.

134

"Maybe it has," Casey conceded, "but without you and Blossom there'll be no waking. A rendezvous of flesh and spirit, that's what Mr C calls it."

"Why me *and* Blossom?" Tom asked, puzzled.

As he put the question, he turned to Blossom herself, but she had climbed one of the grassy banks which enclosed the lane. They clambered up beside her and were greeted by an unobstructed view of the picturesque little village and its harbour, and of the white-capped sea beyond. "Beautiful it may be," Casey said gloomily, "but there's no road for us there."

Blossom waved his objection aside. "Yes, there," she insisted silently, and nodded towards the harbour.

For Tom that simple gesture was like a shadow passing across the brightness of the day, the sunlit scene momentarily eclipsed by a vision of Tower Rock.

"You mean steal a boat?" he asked in a tight voice.

"Wait a minute," Casey objected. "There're no boats down there."

"They'll be back by nightfall," Tom said, remembering with a sudden pang the sound of his father's returning footsteps in the late afternoon, and the smell of the sea he always brought home with him. "Most of them will be, at any rate," he added sadly.

"That's it then!" Casey exclaimed, his mood changing abruptly. "We'll sail back tonight." He let out a crow of triumphant laughter, his face flushed with excitement. "By heck, Tom, we'll fool them. There they'll be, guarding the top of the cliffs for all they're worth, and all the while we'll be sailing like gulls across the water behind them. Why, we'll be up and past them before they think to look over their shoulders."

He performed a jig-like dance on the grassy bank, inviting the others to join in, but neither was in a mood for celebration. Even Blossom seemed daunted by the prospect of the task ahead.

"My, but you're lucky beggars," Casey went on happily. "I'd give my good leg to see the Sleeper in his high tower. Just the once. With him lying there, the way he's done for ages past, waiting for you to make him whole again."

135

"You'll see him if we do," Tom said.

"Don't give me any of your ifs, young Roland," Casey answered, clapping him on the back. "You're the ones for me, you and Blossom both. Between you, you could climb to heaven – which in a manner of speaking is what you *will* be doing. As for me . . ." The excitement died from his face as he suddenly considered his own immediate future. "These eyes of mine will never look on the Sleeper. Nor were they meant to. I'm no great shakes as a climber, as you know. Anyway, that's not what I'm here for. My job is to keep you safe for as long as I can. It's a job I'm content with."

He continued with that role now, by leading them away from the public lane – across a flowered meadow and towards a meandering line of trees that followed the course of a stream. There, after quenching their thirst, they settled down in the speckled shade and prepared to sit out the long hours until nightfall.

Because it was only mid-afternoon, Tom gave no thought to sleep. Yet within minutes he was feeling irresistibly drowsy, just as he had on the previous day; and as on that other occasion the unseen voice began whispering to him. "Lethe . . ." it murmured softly. "Lethe . . .", its beguiling tones oddly in harmony with the gurgle and splash of the nearby stream.

In a brief show of resistance, Tom forced open his eyes and saw that Blossom was already asleep, her face twitching as she entered the Dream. She gave a low moan, whether of distress he could not tell, but loud enough to recall Casey who propped himself up on one elbow and gazed down at her fondly, unaware that he was being observed.

"Goodbye, sweet Blossom," he whispered, and patted her crippled shoulder as if she were a child needing to be comforted.

It was the finality of the whispered endearment that surprised Tom. "Goodbye?" he queried aloud.

Casey gave him a sleepy smile. "Let's face it, Tom, it'll be my turn sooner or later."

"I don't see why . . ." Tom began, but Casey cut him short.

"Jack's had one go at me," he said, fingering his cheek. "Second time round I may not be so lucky. If I can hold him off long enough for you and Blossom to get through, then like I said before, I'll be content. What happens to me won't matter."

"It'll matter to Blossom," Tom reminded him. "And to me, too."

"You're forgetting something, Tom," Casey said with a soft chuckle. "No parting is forever. Wake the Sleeper, and we'll all be together again." He let himself sink back into the straggly grass. "Ah, yes," he sighed drowsily, "everything will be all right then. This old leg of mine will mend. Blossom'll stand as straight as any lass in the town. And your Pa will come sailing . . . sailing . . ." He sighed once more as he also slipped away.

Tom, alone in the spring-bright morning, stared up through the criss-cross of branches and leaves that sheltered them. Was Casey right? he wondered. If he and Blossom were successful, would everything revert to what it had been? Or become even better? Would his father really sail back into his life? He shook his head. He could not allow himself to believe that. The first loss had been bad enough. Having to live through it yet again . . . that would be unbearable. Lacking Casey's simple faith, all he could do was try and hold to the one thing that had sustained him so far – to the child. The rest – the nature of the Dream, the identity of the Sleeper, the golden promises – might possibly be no more than a sad trick played on them all. But the child! That *had* to be true. (Hadn't it?)

There, so near the end of his journey, he struggled to fend off the worst doubt of all: that the child itself might not be what it seemed. No! He shook his head for the second time. He wouldn't let himself think that. The hope conveyed by the child's fluttering eyes, by its golden halo of hair, that hope *had* to be real.

But hope for what? Not for his father who, sadly, was dead and gone. Then for whom? The answer came to him in the form of a single name. Blossom. She was his one real hope now. He admitted it without reserve.

If their journey together delivered Blossom to him – that and nothing else – he would be satisfied.

He turned his head to look at her and was pained to see how distressed she seemed, her features contorted by grief. Hastily, he closed his eyes, willing himself to join her, and straight away the drowsiness returned. As did the voice. "She needs you," it whispered enticingly. "We both do." Voice and stream entwining once again, carrying him free of the sunlight.

17 He could tell from the droop of her shoulders that she needed him. Her face below the blindfold was bruised with anguish, her cheeks hollowed out by the green-tinted darkness. Casey was kneeling beside her in the gloom, his forehead pressed to the snow, his unvoiced song raised in lament.

"Lost!" he keened, his grief ringing high and soulful through the brittle air. "Gone!"

Groping his way to the threshold, Tom stepped across, into a scene of desolation. The nearer of the two hovels, the one which had refused them entry, had been completely destroyed. Fragments of wall and roof littered the snow all around, as if something had descended from the sky and torn it apart. The same hideous force had also turned on the other hovel. Except that there it had confined itself to a small portion of the snow-covered roof, directly above the child's resting place, where there was a gaping hole.

"Lost!" Casey continued, his song more chilling than the freezing night in which they huddled. "Gone!"

"No!" Tom shouted, his denial so strident and loud that it split the black sky, allowing through a jagged burst of light.

Before the sky had closed, he was running across the trampled snow, butting past the leather flap at the doorway and into the hovel's dimly-lit interior. All the inmates were there as before, but now transfixed by fear. The hawk frozen to its perch; the cows utterly motionless, their eyes more moonlike than ever; the people flattened against the far wall, their lips drawn back in a horrified grin.

"What happened?" Tom yelled, causing the house to shudder, the two people to fall to the ground, gibbering insanely.

139

He leapt over them, grazing his head on a roof-beam, and stumbled, dazed, into the storeroom. Expecting nothing, less than nothing: a desolation more complete than anything he had witnessed outside. Instead, he discovered a scene that was barely credible. An untidy hole punched through the hard-packed snow of the ceiling. The floor strewn with razor fragments of shattered icicle. One wall raked by claw-marks. And in the midst of all – the child. Magically unharmed, untouched by the destructive fury that had swept down upon the hovels, it was sleeping peacefully, as if protected by an invisible ring of enchantment.

Tom snatched it up and pressed it against him; buried his face in the folds of its neck and breathed its warm milky smell. So safe it felt. So secure. Not a tremor in its tiny limbs. The rosebud lips, swollen with sleep, puffed outwards after each breath. Even as he held it close, its outflung hand grasped once, compulsively, at the empty air, and on finding nothing, slowly opened again, like a flower of promise.

Awed by its presence, by the mystery of its survival, Tom carried it through the hut and out to where Casey was still kneeling in the snow. When he saw the child in Tom's arms, he leapt up, his lament rising to a peal of joy. Blossom detected the change in his song immediately. Her composure breaking under the impact of relief, she forgot herself long enough to grope blindly towards Tom and to kiss him on the cheek. Her lips startlingly soft, tender, like petals brushing his skin. He swung around expectantly, but the joyous moment had passed. She had already reverted to her usual state of sullen withdrawal; her masked face turned pointedly to the icy tower that glimmered through the darkness.

It was a directive he could not ignore. Stifling his disappointment – her continued rejection of him as mysterious as the survival of the child – he lifted the pack to his shoulders and settled it comfortably. That done, they all three set out on the last leg of their journey.

With Casey leading Blossom by the hand, they trudged off through a night so cold that the frost gathered thick on their eyebrows and lashes and on the fine down around their mouths; the air so raw that it rasped their throats and left a dull ache deep in their lungs. To keep warm they had to stamp their feet at every step; lap their arms repeatedly against their

140

chests – their faces, all the while, enveloped in clouds of breathy vapour that obscured everything but the image of the tower. Always that remained in view, in spite of the blackness of the night; in spite of the brief flurries of hard, grainy snow that lashed their already numb faces. Brushing the half frozen rheum from their eyes, they would find it there before them: a starfall from the starless heavens; a spear of greenish light that twinkled frostily, luring them on.

Compared with the hard purity of the tower, the settlement was like a blasphemy. An ugly blemish even in that wasteland. The straggle of outlying huts, shadowy against the dull gleam of snow, spoke not just of poverty, but of disease and death. From an open doorway there came the sound of a racking cough, followed by a childlike wail. Pinched faces, gaunt with hunger and misery, stared out at them from other makeshift dwellings. A broken-down horse, skeletally thin and protected only by a tattered leather covering, stood in the discoloured snow, its head drooping almost to the ground. Casey went over to pat it, but it shied stiffly away, eyes rolling, long yellow teeth exposed.

There was a cackle of laughter and a short misshapen figure, ragged beyond description, hobbled towards them bearing a smoky torch. In the uncertain light they saw it was a man – unshaven and with rubbery lips and only one eye that fixed upon them cunningly. Dragging off his hood, he bowed low, greasy hair falling about his face, and said something in his own strange language. When they made no reply, he scampered over to the nearest dwelling and tore a carving of the bird-creature from above the doorway. Instantly the doors of nearby houses slammed shut, leather flaps were pulled hurriedly across exposed entrances. Again he cackled with laughter and yelled out what sounded like a challenge. Then, holding the carving high, so it caught the full light of the torch, he carried it triumphantly back to Tom as though it were a precious offering.

"Keep away!" Tom growled, his words leaving glittering trails upon the dark.

The man leered and stepped closer, confident of the power of the carving, and Tom lashed out wildly, catching him across the side of the head. He showed no sign of resenting the blow. He seemed almost to accept it as his due, because he dropped to his knees and tried to kiss Tom's feet.

"I said keep away!" Tom shouted, and this time his words were like starbursts in the silence.

The man rose slowly and shuffled backwards – a few grudging paces, that was all, to show how unwilling he was to leave them. His one eye gleaming craftily, the carving clutched to his chest, he waved the torch in the direction of the tower, as much as to say: "There lies your path". And when they hesitated, he acted as their self-appointed guide, limping on ahead to light the way.

There was nothing they could do to drive him off. Tom tried pushing him roughly aside; and once Casey thwacked him so hard across the back that he was sent sprawling. But apart from making him more servile, their actions had no effect. Always, after cowering down respectfully, he would scurry past them and resume his role as guide. Their ill-treatment of him seemed even to attract some of his fellows, because every so often another shabby figure stole from the shadows to join him.

By the time they had penetrated the outskirts of the settlement there was quite a cavalcade ahead of them – a shambling crowd of men and women whose torches cast a tawdry yellow stain upon the snow. At their approach doors continued to slam; adult voices hastily stilled the cries of frightened children; mangy dogs, their backs hooped with hunger, yelped softly and scuttled off into the night. Yet still the numbers swelled, each new arrival more misshapen than the last. One after the other they presented themselves to Tom before joining the mob, as though seeking his approval. A continuous stream of leering faces, of toothless mouths, of scabbed or pock-marked cheeks, all caught in the flickering torchlight; of grimy hands, bare despite the cold, that clung greedily to winged and taloned carvings.

Casey, ever more troubled by the growing throng, kept glancing across at Tom, silently willing him to do something – anything – that would rid them of these unwanted companions. With the child lying peacefully inside the pack, however, Tom was as unsure how to react as Casey. Because of her blindfold, Blossom was the only one not unsettled by the situation, and whenever Tom or Casey held back, reluctant to go on, she urged them forward, her lips parted eagerly.

They were now well into the settlement. The tower so close that it reared above them, a rod of pale light dividing the blackness of the heavens. Beneath it, radiating outwards from its base, the dense clusters of huts formed an unsightly fringe through which the torch-bearing mob picked its way.

The rough track they were following, ice-hard and deeply rutted, wound steadily down towards a cross-roads where some kind of platform had been erected. Tom was almost upon it before he realised what it was. A gallows, with three bodies dangling lifelessly from its projecting beams. In the wash of light from the torches, he glimpsed the bruised, sightless faces of the dead, their heads lolling forward or fallen sideways in a disturbing mockery of sleep. Above them, splay-legged upon one of the beams, stood a large black bird which cawed noisily. Someone threw a snowball at it, and it launched itself into flight, its gorged body swooping so low that one passing wing-tip almost brushed Tom's cap. There was loud laughter and more snowballs were thrown, this time at the hanging bodies, making them jerk and rotate on their rope halters.

"Stop it!" Tom shouted – and from the direction of the tower was heard a sharp crack, of ice shattering under strain.

Tom looked up, uneasily, towards the very top of the gleaming shaft, to where an array of tendrils swung to and fro, giving off high discordant chimes. Tendrils? Here, where no shrub or tree existed? Or giant icicles, perhaps, suspended from the blind head of the tower like an accumulation of frozen tears?

The mob had grown strangely hushed and still. They were also gazing upwards, silenced by this visible proof that the tower could move; that it was less solid and stable than the ground beneath their feet. As its swaying ceased, they continued their onward march, except that now they were far more subdued. There was no more laughter, no more throwing of snowballs. They held their torches high, for fear of the surrounding dark; their carvings were thrust out before them like shields to ward off some nameless evil.

Other gallows materialized through the gloom: dark angular structures that loomed over the poor dwellings, their grisly burdens reduced to blobs of shadow. More of the birds, black guardians perched on high, cawed a bold challenge to the passing crowd. Their bleak voices made even Blossom falter

143

and draw in close to Tom and Casey. Yet oddly, through it all, the child slept on. Secure within the pack, its peaceful slumber undisturbed by the least twitch or moan.

As the hillside levelled out, they reached the most squalid region of the settlement. Some of the huts were hardly more than windbreaks, their flimsy structures sagging beneath the weight of the taloned carvings that dominated them. Others again were poorer still: mere screens of uncured hide which served as shelter for ragged families. And there was refuse everywhere. Half-gnawed bones and scraps of fur and feathers littered the narrow spaces between the huts. A dead animal, too decayed to be recognisable, lay stretched across the rutted surface of the track.

Here there were no gallows, but in their place woven leather cages hung from poles. The pallid faces of the captives stared hopelessly between the struts; twig-thin arms reached through the gaps in wordless supplication. One of the torch-bearers poked his torch into the nearest cage, driving the captive back, the atmosphere suddenly heavy with the odour of singed hair.

"Leave him!" Tom called.

This second cry was accompanied by another sharp crack, much closer and louder than before. A rifle-shot of splintering ice that caused the whole tower to tremble on its foundations, its light to dim noticeably.

Again the procession paused. Stood silent and watchful in the icy wind. A few of the misshapen guides fell to their knees and waited, heads bowed, faces hidden within their hoods. When nothing more happened – the pale light of the tower slowly returning – they started forward once more. Though now there was murmuring amongst them, their voices raised not in anger, but anticipation. A low babble that grew to a rhythmic chant and kept time to the regular shuffle of their feet.

Blossom had taken Tom and Casey's hands and pulled them both hard against her. Her head was tilted slightly as she listened past the murmured chant to something else: to other voices carried faintly to them on the wind. As the sound of those voices swelled, taking on a distinct note of defiance, so another row of torches, fluttering fireflies of light, showed between the last of the huts.

For the first time in hours the child moved. Kicked vigorously. And Tom, ever sensitive to its needs, dragged Casey and Blossom into the shadow of a nearby hut, allowing the rest of the procession to go on without them. Cautiously, they peered around the side wall towards the base of the tower. It was little more than a stone's throw away, a shaft of pure crystal that slotted into the land's edge. On either side of it, a hard line marked out the top of a cliff; and beyond that all was darkness, though already the sky above was grey-white with the coming dawn.

Yet it was something other than the brightening dawn that forced the grunt of surprise from Tom's lips. Standing guard all along the cliff's edge was a row of sentinels; and hurrying to meet them, an untidy wedge of twisted, shambling figures. Two equal groups, like armies about to clash in open battle, their waving torches, torn by the rising wind, being drawn out into fluttering banners of yellow-white flame.

Anticipating what must happen, Tom began unwinding the rope from about his body. Beside him Blossom clawed away her blindfold, her eyes stretched wide in a desperate effort to see more clearly. And quickly, before she could pull free, he tied the loose end of the rope around her waist, leaving a loop of slack between them.

"What . . .?" she demanded. Not in words. Her high song all but lost as it was whirled away by the wind. "What . . .?"

"There's going to be a fight," he told her quietly.

That was all he needed to say. The rope snapped tight, and he and Casey had to hurry to catch up, all three of them racing for the tower.

A short distance ahead the wedge of advancing bodies, brandishing beaked and taloned carvings like weapons, smashed into the waiting sentinels. There was a confusion of noise and movement. Torches swung wildly, others hissed out as they were trampled into the snow, and all at once a gap appeared in the line: an open portion of clifftop, right beside the tower, onto which the dawn light poured. Tom and Blossom made straight for it and were almost there when a shadow fell across the space, followed by the squat, muscular figure of a man. His hood was thrown back, revealing a clean strong face that could never have originated in the squalor of the settlement; summer-blue eyes that had never probed the darkness of some dingy hovel.

"Here's for you, Tom Roland!" Jack roared, but the tower stood firm, unmoved by his challenge.

Not so Tom. As those strong hands lunged for his throat, he ducked and dodged aside, and Casey stepped into his place, he and Jack resuming their unfinished struggle. Their two powerful bodies slammed together, locked in a conflict so intense that they seemed unaware of how their sliding feet carried them closer and closer to the lip of the cliff. One last slip on the icy surface and they were over. Only Jack, flinging out an arm, managed to save himself, his mittened hand grasping at the cliff's edge and holding on. Of Casey there was no sign. Just the slightest of shudders as, far below, the barren plain received him.

Had it not been for the rope which brought her up short, Blossom would surely have followed him over. Head tipped back, throat distended, she was striving desperately to call out; but no sound emerged, though her lashes sparkled with frozen tears, and it was left to Tom to cry aloud in anguish.

"Casey!"

A drawn-out grieving cry that brought an immediate response from the tower. There was a deafening report, like a cannon going off, and the whole structure reeled and nearly collapsed. It righted itself, but not before many of the giant icicles dangling from its summit had snapped off and come hurtling down.

A hail of icy spears, they fell haphazardly on the warring sides, narrowly missing some people and pinning others to the snow. One long sliver of ice stuck quivering into the ground at Tom's feet, and he wrenched it out and used it as a staff to beat a path to the base of the tower. There he glanced upwards, once, at the glittering shaft; and then, with a strange mixture of sadness and exhilaration, as though this after all was the prize he had sought all his life, he began to climb.

Those first heady minutes were the easiest. Driven on by some inner urge, he somehow found a way up the crystal surface, his hands and feet probing for dents and ridges where they hardly existed. The noise below grew rapidly fainter; the day brightened around him; and gradually, as the last shreds of night dissolved, he became conscious of the peril he was in.

How, he wondered, pausing in mid-movement, could he continue clinging on like this? When there was still so far to go? When, already, he was shaking with strain?

He felt a gentle tug on the rope and he glanced around to find Blossom right there beside him. But how did that help, when she was clearly more tired than he? For whether he looked down or up, he met with the same shimmering vista of mirror-smooth ice.

As his nerve began to fail, he heard the voice. Not Blossom's, nor his own, but that other deeper voice that lived within him. "Climb," it instructed him, and the child yawned and stretched and sighed inside the pack. "Climb. For me."

He tried, but his will failed again, the wind licking hungrily at his cheek and leaving it numb. As numb as his fingertips which ached with the effort of holding on.

"For me . . . for me . . ." the voice murmured enticingly.

But higher, clearer than the voice was Blossom's song. As ever, it contained no words, only an idea. That he should search deeper, deeper, into the crystal heart of the tower.

He pressed his face to the ice, stared into the glittering core . . . and saw it! A jagged flaw that spiralled upwards, its winding path cross-hatched with tiny cracks that ran outwards to the surface.

He ripped off his gloves and felt for one of those cracks now. Located it and felt for another and another – inching his way round and up, his slow progress mapping the spiral of the flaw.

Behind and a little below him, Blossom followed his every move. She paused when he paused; groped for each unseen handhold exactly as he did; mirrored the way he flattened himself against the curved surface whenever the wind plucked at them. She made no mistakes. Despite her damaged body, despite the fatigue which showed in the hollows of her cheeks and in the bruised skin beneath her eyes, her movements remained sure and steady, all her skills as a climber perfectly recalled.

"We'll soon be there," he called encouragingly. "Soon."

And the sky, as if chastening them both, slid open like a shutter onto blackness. Onto a night softened by the glimmer of stars and a warm earth smell.

He blinked, and the pearly-grey sky of morning slid back

into place. So too did the tower, its summit beckoning him on. Yet the blackness, that brief glimpse of star-filled night, had served as a warning which he knew better than to ignore. Leaning outwards, held precariously by his fingertips, he searched for the place of sanctuary which he knew must be hereabouts.

It was just a few handholds away: a narrow opening in the surface of the tower where a fragment of flawed crystal had broken free. He climbed up to it. The inside was like an enchanted grotto, decorated with icy shards that fractured the light into rainbow hues. With Blossom bracing him, he slipped off the pack and placed the child on the one smooth area near the bottom of the opening. It settled into its frozen refuge as he knew it must; its outflung hand, wonderfully dimpled, came to rest only fractionally short of a needle-point of blue-green ice. The very carelessness of its attitude declared, as it always did, that here it harboured no fears, had no further need of protection. The slight twitch of its fingers, the sigh from its pouting lips, were like delicate acts of dismissal.

"Safe," Tom whispered, satisfied, and stepped back.

Into space!

The rope jerked taut, and he and Blossom together were hurtling downwards. "Casey . . . !" he thought despairingly, sharing again in the pain of that other tragic plunge. A heartache that drew him to itself in a shriek of bitter wind . . . or would have done had the sky not changed. Darkened. A black sheet superimposed upon the grey, but dotted now with starlight.

18 The sky steadied above him. Through wind-tossed branches it showed as a wide black meadow flowered with stars. Tom lay there in the blustery night, looking up, aware that he should be contemplating something else – something deeply hurtful and therefore not to be acknowledged. He managed to block it out until Blossom's sobs sounded past the noise of the wind, too loud to be ignored any longer. Then he rolled over, to where Casey was lying stark and still beside them. Casey's stricken features in the starlight were pure elfin, and totally unresponsive to Blossom's wordless cries, her tears falling onto his cheeks and running down as if they were his own.

Tom stood up and eased her gently away, her face only slightly less elfin than Casey's.

And Tom's own face? Was that also . . .? The thought flitted across his mind and he accepted it. Yes, after Casey's sacrifice, this was how it should be. For both of them. Waking or sleeping, they belonged now to the child.

"Come," he murmured, and led her away from the trees, out into a night of approaching storm; a portion of sky, over to their right, already empty of stars.

She followed him without protest, though for some minutes she continued to vent her grief in half-stifled sobs. Only once was she almost overcome, and he waited at a respectful distance while she crouched in the grass, her shoulders heaving with emotion. After that she made no further complaint, her tear-stained face as stern as its elfin features would allow.

They approached the village from along the shore so as to avoid the narrow streets where even at night there was a chance of encountering passers-by. Unseen, they reached the inner wall of the harbour which was fronted by the glowing lights of the tavern. On a night such as this, the tavern door was firmly shut, and they crept safely past, their footsteps masked by the murmur of voices and occasional snatches of song.

Now they were stealing along the stone jetty that angled out into the rising surf. On its landward side, in the protected waters of the harbour, was moored a long line of boats. Tom, who had learned about the sea from his father, ran his eye over each of them in turn, looking for something small and manageable. He soon found what he was after: a short beamy craft, for stability; quarter-decked, to keep out the breaking seas; and with a single mast stepped forward of the covered hold. It had one further advantage that Tom had not thought of: its furled sails were dark-coloured and less likely to be noticed.

While Blossom slipped the moorings, Tom half-raised the mainsail. It snapped full as the wind caught it, and immediately they were in motion, scraping and jostling past the boats on either side. Tom leapt for the tiller in time to prevent any serious collision, and seconds later they were winging across the harbour towards the entrance. Behind them the tavern door crashed open and a group of revellers staggered out, but they were far too engrossed in their drunken song to notice the small craft speeding away, its dark sail almost invisible against the backdrop of the night.

After the relative calm of the harbour, the open sea met them with a series of hammer-blows. Wave upon wave broke across their bow, driving the nose under and nearly swamping them. With Tom clinging to the tiller and Blossom bailing as hard as she could, they somehow survived that first onslaught and made their way out into deeper water where the seas were less steep. There they drove rapidly between the long swells, the sail straining, the sturdy craft heeled half over under the constant pressure of the wind.

From all that his father had told him, Tom knew that they needed to be well clear of land before the storm arrived. To that end he sailed straight out from the shore, holding to his course even when the side rail disappeared beneath the surge and the rigging sang out in protest. At their backs the lights from the village dwindled to a faint glow; while up ahead the hard angry line of advancing cloud blotted out the stars one by one.

The first real gust of the storm struck with incredible force, laying the vessel over on its side and spilling them into the sea. As he floundered helplessly, half smothered by the foam, it came to Tom that this perhaps was the grim truth behind the Sleeper's promise. Here, in the storm's cruel heart, was where he was destined to meet again with his father, in a last enduring reunion. He took a spluttering breath, intending to scream out a refusal, and then Blossom's hand closed around his and she was tugging him back onto the steeply sloping deck.

Slowly the boat righted itself. Only to be met by another gust that bent the mast to its limit. Just when it seemed about to break, there was a loud bang and the sail blew out, leaving behind only a few shreds of madly flapping canvas. That was what saved them. That, and the speed with which Tom swung the tiller. Shuddering but still upright, the boat turned from the wind and ran bare-poled before the mounting storm.

There was no question of steering in any particular direction. Especially when the rain started: a brief deluge that scoured the salt from their clothes and bodies and swept the decks clean. Half blinded by it, all Blossom and Tom could do was hold on, their arms clamped to the tiller as the boat bucked and swung beneath them.

The rain did not last long, though even when it stopped they could see almost nothing. Surrounded by high seas and with the stars obscured, the only glimmer of light came from the faint luminescence given off by the churned water in their wake. And that light, ghostly and insubstantial, was too reminiscent of the green-tinted darkness in the Dream to be comforting. Drenched and shivering with cold in the strong wind, their one real comfort lay in their nearness to each other; in the close touch of their hands on the tiller.

Like most spring storms, it passed in a few hours. Thereafter, although the wind dropped to a stiff breeze and the stars reappeared, the seas stayed high; and now, without any sail or storm to drive it forward, the boat wallowed in the deep troughs, the following waves looming dangerously over the stern. Sooner or later, as Tom realised only too well, one of those waves would break and swamp them.

After a particularly narrow escape – the boat teetering on a crest which hissed menacingly as it slid past – Tom left Blossom at the tiller and felt his way forward. In the locker under the decked section he found a staysail which he set as best he could in the dark. It was too small to give them much speed through the water, but at least it kept them clear of the troughs, the boat now butting sluggishly into the long swells.

Also in the locker he found an emergency water ration, and he shared this and the last of the soggy food with Blossom. Afterwards they remained together in the stern, though by then only one of them was needed to steer – Blossom choosing to curl up close beside him, her hand, under cover of darkness, reaching out surreptitiously for his.

In an odd kind of way that was a happy time for Tom. And, he suspected, for Blossom too. A lull between two stormy passages. The real storm behind them; the storming of Tower Rock still to come. But not yet. This inbetween time was theirs alone. An hour or two, that was all – for by Tom's own reckoning it was already past midnight – yet all the more precious for that reason. Now, in this brief period divorced from past and future, he fully acknowledged the strength of emotion that bound him to the girl at his side. The warm pressure of her hand, the easy silence that existed between them, these simple things he accepted as an expression of all that he desired most. There was no need for words. Words could only have betrayed him: either by falling short of what he felt; or, far worse, by inviting a possible rebuff – something which, all at once, he feared more even than he feared the Rock.

Not that he sat there idly. Despite the nature of his feelings, he remained watchful and alert. The occasional shore lights, glimpsed from the highest crests, enabled him to work out roughly where they were; from the pattern of the stars he gauged their overall direction; and when the distant glow of the town lights first appeared, he moved the tiller without any prompting from Blossom and swung the boat in towards the shore.

With the wind now blowing across their beam, they made good time. Gradually the glow from the town grew stronger, a brightening beacon that might almost have been placed there to guide them in. He steered straight for it, aware all the while of Blossom's grip tightening in his, the tension mounting steadily. Until, with a shock of recognition, they saw what they were searching for. The Rock! A lightless band in the midst of the town's glow. A smudge of murky shadow that stood like a point of menace between them and the stars.

The boom of the surf was loud in their ears before Blossom withdrew her hand. She did so reluctantly, in order to grope her way forward to the locker. She returned with a coil of rope which she knotted first around Tom's waist and then around her own. The two of them tied together as they had been in the Dream; their twin fates finally conjoined.

"We're nearly there!" Tom cried out in warning.

Unnecessarily, because the luminous lines of surf stretching away on either side were clear to see. A wave lifted them high and carried them towards the black wall of the cliff; towards Tower Rock which, like a dark blade, split the sky from zenith to horizon.

Yet now, for all their fear of the Rock, it was impossible for them to look up, the immediate dangers of the surf demanding all their attention. Falling off one wave, they were caught in the trough of the next – only to be slammed broadside-on and all but capsized as they were driven forward in a welter of foam. From the corner of his eye Tom detected something paler than the dark water. A ribbon of sand, glimpsed and then gone. He clambered hastily to his feet, but Blossom was quicker. Already she was standing at the stern, urging him to join her, the two of them leaping clear an instant before the boat struck the beach and split apart.

They landed in the shallows, where the backwash dragged at their ankles as they scrambled for the cliff. They had climbed no more than a metre or two when a fresh wave roared in. Smashing onto the sand below, it surged up over their heads and they had to brace themselves against the cliff. As the water began to recede, a piece of debris from the wreck caught Tom in the side, partially winding him. He tried to take a breath, but drew water into his lungs instead, and the shock of it made him lose his hold. Choking and coughing, he felt himself being plucked free, dragged outwards by the tide; but the rope jerked and held, and Blossom, her body wedged in a cleft of rock, was hauling him in. She reached out for him greedily, her hands more possessive than the sea, her arms encircling his chest, refusing to release him until the waters relented and withdrew.

Other waves followed, but by then they were well clear, engaged in the first and far less treacherous part of the climb. The real challenge of Tower Rock would come later, up beyond the cliff-top, where the Rock truly began. For the present all they had to contend with was a normal section of cliff, its weathered surface offering no great difficulty, even in the dark. If they had any immediate concern, it was not so much for themselves as for the many roosting birds, which once disturbed might easily alert anyone watching from above.

With that in mind, they took particular pains not to trample the nests, working carefully from ledge to ledge until soon they were high above the crashing surf. Then, in a moment of carelessness, Tom let his hand brush a nesting bird. There was a loud squawk, and he felt the jab of a beak against his forearm. Wings beat about his shoulders, accompanied by more noisy squawking.

"Who's there?" a voice called out.

Slightly above him and over to his left, where the cliff-top met the base of the Rock, a lamp appeared. Suspended from a long pole, it swung out into space, casting its light directly onto him and Blossom.

"It's them!" the same voice declared excitedly.

And someone else: "I'll fetch Jack!"

Footsteps clattered off into the night, and the fugitives, making the most of the light as well as the delay, climbed for all they were worth.

A fierce tug of wind told them when they were level with the cliff-top – the wind always so much stronger here where the land flattened out – and soon afterwards their groping fingers encountered the glassy-smooth surface which marked the beginning of Tower Rock.

Earlier, out on the open sea, Tom had half believed he was ready for this moment; but now, confronted by it, he was suddenly overcome by dread. By a mindless, stultifying terror. Feeling for his previous handhold, he pressed himself against the cliff, allowing Blossom to inch past. Blossom! Who had already fallen once and was supposed to be following his lead. His! He felt the rope tighten between them and he tried to clamber after her. Tried . . . and failed. Too terrified to move. Frozen there by the thought of what would surely happen if he dared to venture higher. The same fate awaiting him as all the other hardy souls who had pitted their skills against the Rock in years gone by. Legendary climbers every one of them, but consigned to an early grave just the same. Their lives ended abruptly on the reef below.

Somewhere overhead Blossom was whimpering for him to follow, but already it was too late. He had never freely chosen this task, and now, confronted by it, he could not find within himself either the necessary courage or resolve. After all, what was he climbing towards? Who *was* the Sleeper? A dark figure from a monstrous past – kin to the bird-creature perhaps – or the age-old saviour Mr Crawford would have him be? Which?

Footsteps – many of them – clattered back along the cliff-top; more lamps swung out on either side of the Rock. On the ledges all around him the nesting birds were blinking sleepily, their eyes stained tawny-yellow by the lamplight. Tom turned his head to where a knot of people had gathered only metres from where he stood, their voices just audible above the whistle of the wind.

"Shall we try and bring him in?" he heard a woman ask.

"No, there's a better way." That was Jack, his voice abrupt and authoritative. And then, much louder: "Tom, can you hear me? I know you're not interested in anything I have to say, but there's someone else here. Someone you'd do well to hearken to."

One of the lanterns was lifted higher, and Tom saw his mother's face in the crowd, tear-stained and distraught.

"Come down, Tom," she pleaded. "For our sakes if not for your own."

It was not a plea he could easily dismiss, and again he tried to move – not up nor down nor even sideways –

his sole desire, as yet, simply to gain control of his own limbs, to shake off this trance of dread that held him captive. But still the thought of the Rock bore down upon him, a dark weight that pinned him to the ledge.

"Please, Tom!" she wailed.

He forced his mouth to work, the words coming out tight and hard. "I can't!"

He meant only that he was stuck there, but Jack, convinced he was refusing to come down, pushed Mrs Roland roughly aside.

"If I have to, I'll climb out there and prise you loose!" he shouted. "The Rock's not for you or anyone. D'you hear?"

He heard, though still he could not move.

"Is this how it's to be then?" Jack bellowed, losing all patience, and he snatched up a small figure at his side.

A dwarf? A doll perhaps? Tom strained to see through the dancing shadows – the lanterns tossing to and fro in a wind which had begun to pipe up now that dawn was near. A shaft of soft light settled briefly on a tiny face, revealing it as Denny's, his arms and legs jerking wildly as Jack held him out over the edge of the cliff.

"Leave him be!" Mrs Roland was shouting, her fists pummelling Jack's head and shoulders.

Other hands dragged her away.

"So what's it to be?" Jack demanded. "That Dream-child of yours or this real live one? Look at him, Tom, your own kin, a flesh-and-blood creature like yourself. Would you have the Rock claim him as well? Would you give him up for that monstrous child you've been carrying? Aye, monstrous, Tom, believe me. Don't be fooled by its human shape or its beauty. Behind those closed eyes, there's a being as ugly as any demon from hell. Is that what you'd choose above your own brother? An inhuman thing more unkind than the Rock itself? Than the . . . ?"

Tom never had to make the choice being offered him. Before Jack could finish, Denny twisted around and bit him on the wrist. With an oath, Jack jerked his arms back, and Denny squirmed free and ran for the safety of his mother's skirts.

"Don't listen to him, Tom!" he shrilled. "There's nothing special about his old Rock. It's just a piece of stone."

It was not only Denny's fearlessness, but also the childlike simplicity of his message which finally broke through the spell that bound Tom to the cliff face. ". . . just a piece of stone." Yes, he thought, that and nothing more. A stone like any other. As he, Tom, would prove once and for all. Now! And reaching up, he slowly began to climb again.

Beneath him he could hear fragments of an argument going on between his mother and Jack.

". . . never have dropped him . . . must know that . . ."

". . . nothing of the kind . . . a demon, Jack Steele . . ."

"If it's demons you're after, then cast your eyes up . . ."

". . . frighten me with your stories . . . when my dear son . . ."

Their angry, worried voices, snatched away by the wind, were soon left behind. As were the black-clad climbers, sent out by Jack, who tried in vain to intercept him. Climbing with a new assurance, he moved up past Blossom, who was struggling now as much with her own waning strength as with the Rock; up towards a narrow shelf, fingertip wide, which gave him one of his few chances to rest.

He grasped it with both hands, while behind him the dawn spread across sea and sky, the first grey light revealing how far he still had to go. The Tower far higher than even he had imagined, and more daunting. So tall and dark that he could not take his eyes from it; its blind summit, brushed by tufts of cloud, seemingly unattainable.

That same sight, added to her weakness, was too much for Blossom who let out a faint whimper and lost her hold. Tom heard her cry and felt the rope cut into his waist, his shoulder joints cracking as they took the extra weight. Looking down between his feet, he saw her dangling helplessly in space, her body etched against the corrugated surface of the sea. She was not trying to swing in towards the Tower, as he had expected. Her eyes dull with defeat, she was fumbling with the knot at her waist, trying to untie it.

"I'll follow you if you fall!" he screamed down to her.

She shook her head, still plucking at the rope.

"I'll not go on without you!" he added desperately. "I swear it!"

The passion in his voice must have convinced her because she nodded reluctantly and groped for the cliff face. Her movements sluggish with fatigue, she regained her hold and eased the deadening weight on his shoulders.

They resumed their climb soon afterwards, but five minutes later she fell again, too weak to resist the mounting pressure of the wind. This time it was only by good luck that Tom had a secure hold and was able to support her.

Hanging there she mouthed single word – "Please . . ." – begging him to let her go.

He could not bear even to consider it. "No!" he shrieked, louder than the wind; as defiant as Denny, though he knew in his heart that the odds were heavily against them. For he had only to glance down, to see her struggling feebly at the rope's end, to realize that she could not go on punishing her damaged body for much longer. Nor, if she continued to fall, could he hope to go on saving them both. Eventually one of those sharp jolts of the rope would occur when he was between holds, and then . . . and then . . . He tried to block out the picture that sprang to mind, but it was too vivid – both of them clawing ineffectually at empty space and, far below, the metallic glint of an unyielding sea waiting to receive them. Even now his shoulders were aching almost beyond endurance, his hands white-knuckled, his nails rimmed with blood.

"Hurry!" he sobbed, and pressed his face to the

unfeeling surface of the Tower. Just as he had in the Dream. The cold shock of the stone on his sweating forehead so like the Dream that it brought back to him those other parallel events.

In the Dream, he recalled, there had been no words. Only Blossom's timbrous song, which had urged him to gaze into the Tower's crystalline heart. Where . . . ! – he could hardly contain his relief – where a jagged flaw, surrounded by a spoked halo of cracks, had spiralled from base to summit!

"The Tower! It's flawed!" he sang out, giving back to her in words her original gift to him. A clear note of triumph in his voice that carried down to the anxious-eyed spectators on the cliff-top; that roused the birds from their nests and sent them winging out and up through the breaking day. Up to where Blossom was already feeling for those tiny fractures in the stone which, although too narrow to be seen, were just rough-edged enough to be grasped; the same series of slanting cracks that had saved them once and would save them again.

Moments later, the birds fluttering excitedly about their heads, both she and Tom were moving again, set upon the long spiralling ascent which followed faithfully that path taken by their Dream selves.

When they reached the cleft in the Tower's side, they sensed immediately the child's presence. By day, the hole itself was no more than a ragged tear, blotched with mildew and salt. Still there was no mistaking the ghostly outline that nestled in one of its shadowy corners. The birds seemed to sense it too because they sheered away with raucous cries of alarm that made Tom doubt anew the purpose of this desperate assault on the summit. What if Jack were right? What if the child were really an inhuman thing that . . . ?

But it was too late for such thoughts now. Too many lives had been sacrificed in order to bring them this far, Casey's not the least of them.

"I wish Casey could see us now," Tom observed wistfully, and regretted having spoken as Blossom winced and turned her head in swift denial.

Casey's memory, having once been invoked, could not easily be dismissed. Throughout the remainder of the climb it was as if he were there with them, an invisible third companion. For Tom, Casey's distinctive Dream-song seemed to find an echo in the birds that hovered protectively overhead. He was no less real to Blossom, for when she fell yet again, just short of the summit, it was his name that caused her to rally.

"We can't fail Casey now!" Tom called as she hung listlessly from the rope, all her energy spent. "Not after what he did for us!"

Although she shot him a look of bitter reproach, somehow she tapped into some inner reserve that enabled her to scrabble feebly at the underside of the overhang; to hold on just tight and long enough for Tom to complete the climb.

That last part of the ascent – having to creep out beneath the overhang and up the blind face of the summit – was the hardest thing Tom ever did. Surrounded by milling birds, almost buoyed up by the close pressure of their winged and feathered bodies, he reached at last one of the two narrow slits on the Tower's seaward side. His hands torn and bloodied, his whole body trembling uncontrollably, he tumbled inside. Though still he did not rest. Bracing his feet against the inner wall, he pulled hand-over-hand at the rope until Blossom, her face paler than the morning sky, crawled in beside him.

For a while they were too spent to do more than lie there; but as their pounding hearts slowed, they sat up and surveyed what all their efforts had brought them to. Not a splendid chamber, nor even a simple cell. Far removed from the living roar of the sea, this was an unutterably dank and dreary place, its only sound the dull plunk of dripping water. Ill-lit by the two slit windows, closed-off and musty, it conveyed the hopeless atmosphere of a dungeon buried deep in the earth.

As with the cleft lower down, its floor was blotched with damp and mildew; its walls and ceiling festooned with hanging crystals of salt that had long since lost their sparkle and shine. Grown dull and grey with age, they sprouted from the rock like cancerous growths.

Pools of shadow obscured the furthest extremities of the room, but nearer at hand Tom and Blossom could just make out some kind of raised platform. And stretched across it, a long irregular shape.

Nervously they drew nearer. As their eyes became accustomed to the gloom, they saw that the platform was in fact a stone couch, and that the shape upon it was the gigantic figure of a sleeping man. A man as old as he was huge. His massive limbs, more ancient and craggy than the Tower, might have been carved from flint. His once elfin features, seamed and creased by untold years, bore the same stony quality, the mouth and eyes chiselled closed. His clothing, in the form of a long leather tunic, had all but mouldered away, the few remaining shreds, brittle and discoloured, allowing the corpse-grey skin to show through. Yet he was not dead. Periodically he groaned in his sleep and jerked at the manacle which bound his outflung arm to the wall. Encountering resistance from the heavy chain, his hand, strangely claw-like, would sink back beside his hairless skull. The hand, the head, the vast limbs and body, then remained gripped by rocky stillness until the Dream set his eyelids aquiver and his hand and arm went into spasm once again.

Awed, and also intrigued by this strange spectacle, Tom and Blossom peered closely at the upturned face, trying to decipher the character written there; but with the eyes closed, those petrified features told them little of the mind that lay within. Mustering their courage, they crept nearer still. Close enough for Tom to reach out and touch the horny sole of one foot with his fingertips. It was freezing cold, an icy current running from the foot, up Tom's arm, and down to the fossilized scale hidden in his pocket. With a shudder, he jerked his hand away, his whole body chilled by the brief contact.

"What is it?" Blossom asked silently, seeing how he shivered and hunched his shoulders against the bitter cold that clutched at him.

He did not know what to tell her; did not understand what had just happened. "I . . . I touched the Dream," he stammered. "I mean I . . . I felt it."

But what part of it? That was the question. One he could not yet answer, though already a very real seed of misgiving had taken root in his mind. He could feel it growing there, a fear as chilling as the touch of that horny foot. Which warned him that he had made a terrible mistake; that this elfin giant was no kindly ruler from a loving past; and that he, Tom, should do anything rather than remain here in the chamber, anything rather than fall asleep.

He would have responded to the warning if he had been able to, but he was bone weary after the ordeal of the storm and the long climb. Even with the rope to help him, he could not have faced the perilous descent. Not now. Taking Blossom's hand, he accompanied her back across the chamber, as far from the Sleeper as they could get, to a patch of floor beneath one of the slit windows. There, with a troubled chorus of bird-cries faint in the background, they lay down together for what Tom sensed would be the last time.

19 He could sense them there, somewhere high above, waiting uneasily in a wash of clear light. Impatient to join them, he moved closer to the opening. Here below, the only light came from the pale wand of the Tower. All else was darkness, including the gulf beyond the threshold. Clenching his teeth, he stepped through, onto the Tower's glittering side, his feet lodging on the lower edge of the cleft. That first step, which was the hardest, was like choosing a path that led only upwards; a path he somehow felt compelled to follow.

Though not immediately. First there was the child to be attended to, its tiny body nestled in the jewelled hollow at his feet. A baby still, but with a suggestive hint of wisdom in its quivering eyelids. And charmed anew by the elfin quality of its sleeping face, by the spring-sweet breath, he reached down . . .

. . . and hesitated.

Something about its attitude – so placid except for the occasional twitch of its outflung hand – tugged at his memory. As did the icy breeze that slid beneath his jacket, a finger of pure winter probing for his heart. What was it he had vowed not to forget? What had he meant to bring with him across the threshold? Some hint of danger, some warning voice, telling him not to . . . not to . . . As he searched for the lost thought, the faintest of tremors passed through the Tower, making him sway dangerously. He put a hand to the side of the cleft, to steady himself, and out of the tense silence a voice spoke to him. The same voice he had heard before, but with a new note of urgency in it.

"Don't fail us. You who are the Carrier, stay with us to the end . . . the end . . ."

"The end of what?" he asked aloud, a spume of glistening vapour bursting from his mouth. While behind him, at that precise moment, Blossom stepped trustingly through the portal and missed her footing.

He made a desperate grab for her, the sudden weight wrenching at his shoulder and threatening to tear him loose. He grasped blindly with his other hand and located the sleeping child, its twitching fingers closing ice-hard about his wrist. All three of them bound together like links in a chain, with Blossom suspended below.

"You see," the voice added, whispering intimately to him as Blossom scrambled to safety. "We need each other. All three of us."

After that reminder of how vulnerable they were, he made no further attempt to argue with the voice. For the present he accepted the notion that he had come here for one purpose only: to perform the duties of the Carrier. So that when Blossom stooped for the child, he half turned and allowed her to slip the pack onto his shoulders. Then, roped together, they addressed themselves to the rest of the climb.

Now there was little room in his mind for anything but the task at hand. All his attention focussed on resisting the pressure of the wind, on seeking out those minute fractures in the Tower's surface which alone guaranteed a safe passage. Even had he been free to look down, he would have seen nothing. The two warring groups of people, the impoverished settlement with its squalor and misery, the vastness of the barren plain, all were hidden by the night. For him, now, the only thing that mattered was the Tower; this one path of green-tinted light which thrust up through the gloom; which he had chosen freely (had he not?) and must pursue to . . .

. . . to the end?

Those words, an echo from the immediate past, distracted him momentarily, and for the second time a tremor ran through the Tower. A little stronger than before, it caused one of the icicles dangling from the summit to snap off and plummet down. So close to the Tower's shaft that it grazed his cheek and left behind a thin red line. A warning? (He frowned and brushed away the crystals of frozen blood with the back of his hand.) Or had it been a timely reminder that he could not afford to let his mind wander? Not now, with Blossom growing steadily weaker. For even above the mournful cough of the wind he could hear her laboured breaths; and when he glanced between his feet he could see her face tense with strain, the hollows of her eyes as black as the gulf beneath.

Her obvious distress served to make him both more determined and also more careful. No hand- or foothold was abandoned unless he had a sure grip higher up; and at all times he was braced for that sharp jolt of the rope which could come at any second. Surprisingly it did not occur until they were almost at the summit. From somewhere out beyond the darkness there was a chorus of warning cries, and as he flattened himself against the unyielding crystal, she fell. Not far. The rope was short enough for him to see her face etched cruelly against the black surround: a pale oval of life, of warmth, which gave meaning to the appalling emptiness of the night.

"Don't give up!" he screamed, a starburst of sound that cascaded down upon her in glittering droplets.

Within the pack, the child sighed and turned contentedly, as though reminding him of its presence, and he called less certainly: "Think of . . . think of the . . ." He had intended to remind her of the child, but the word refused to come out, obstructed by the unexpected image of Casey – Casey's face overlaying the child's, eclipsing it temporarily. He tried again, and this time the inner voice insinuated itself into his, using him to transmit thoughts and feelings not his own. "Think of why you are here," he instructed her dispassionately. "Of what you must do. You alone!"

Whatever was meant, it succeeded in reviving her. Kicking feebly, she swung in towards the security of the Tower and climbed slowly up towards him. Though now her face was averted, as if unwilling to meet his eyes; and when he reached out to reassure her, she shuddered and avoided his touch. "What is it?" he asked, baffled by her sudden coolness, his words arching visibly between them.

Her only answer was to point to the forest of icicles, boughless and leafless, which hung from the summit.

Clambering in amongst them, he felt he was entering an enchanted grove. All around him the night was filled with their greenish glow and with the high song struck from them by the wind. As he shifted his weight the individual notes of that song became more shrill and unlovely, rising to a demented shriek whenever he faltered or let his grip slacken.

He paused once, to rest, and noticed how his bare hands were strangely warm. Warm? Despite their contact with the ice? Alert, his suspicions aroused, he looked up and saw that the icicles were not really a part of the Tower at all. They were suspended a fraction below the overhang. Floating in space! As if placed there for a purpose. An illusion designed to convince him . . . of what? That perhaps he was not really . . . ?

Before he could give definite form to his troubled thoughts, the wind moaned, setting the whole grove into motion; raising the pitch of the song to an insane howl that could not be sustained. Spears of ice were snapping off on every side; others were splintering or coming loose in his hands. But there was another song, too, just audible beneath the jangle and crash of breaking ice. Blossom's. Spurred on by it, he swung hazardously around the lip of the summit and up to the narrow slit set into the Tower's crystal mask.

Inside there was total silence. The moan of the wind, the thrum of high song, both were blocked out, replaced by an atmosphere of such breathless calm that he lacked the nerve to turn and examine what he had come to. At his back he could feel the child stirring, waking, and while he still had time he pulled at the rope and kept on pulling until, hollow-eyed with exhaustion, Blossom stood beside him. He heard her draw her breath in sharply – from shock? joy? – and only then did he turn and look.

He too could not stifle that first gasp of surprise. The chamber before him was like something fashioned from the stuff of fairytale. The walls were built from blocks of rain-bowed crystal; the floor and ceiling shot through with the light of unseen stars. Great jewelled clusters hung from every nook and cranny, catching and reflecting the starlight until the very air danced and glowed.

Tom closed his eyes, dazzled by it all, and when he looked again the room was even richer, fuller, peopled with presences from another more golden time. Near at hand he could just detect the silvery outline of two resting figures. Himself? Blossom? How was that possible? These were wondrous elfin creatures, their upturned faces charged with a secret radiance.

Yet for all their other-worldly quality, they were mere pale copies of the sleeping form which reclined upon a couch further into the chamber: a man of gigantic proportions, but imbued with all the crystalline beauty of the tower, as though fashioned from stardust. Only his silhouette was discernible, a gleaming halo within which dwelt a being of untold promise: with a mind wise enough to repair all loss; a heart compassionate enough to heal all wounds; a soul benevolent enough to give comfort wherever it was needed. He lay stretched out on his back, wonderfully still except for one hand which was half raised in a vague gesture of welcome.

Tom yearned to draw nearer, to wake him with a touch, even with a kiss; but instinct warned him that the one sure road to this fabulous being lay through the sleeping couple on the floor. That was why they were placed there. To act as a means of passage, as a bridge between the sleeping and the waking worlds. And with the child whimpering excitedly, its hands and feet clambering against the restriction of the pack, he and Blossom approached the two ghostly figures.

They met with no resistance, but slipped easily, effortlessly, into the fleshy shells of these other identities, like a key entering a lock and turning smoothly. As the lock clicked over – their fingertips tingling in final union with themselves – so the light in the chamber dimmed . . . blurred . . . and . . .

. . . and when they stood up the room was different. Complete in every detail, but overlaid with a gloomier, far more forbidding image of itself – the illusion of the Dream shattered forever. Only a glimpse of the rain-bowed walls remained, their soft sparkle dimmed by dank slabs of stone. The glitter of starlight had been reduced to a heavy dungeon atmosphere. Grey accumulations of salt hung down where once there had been crystal clusters.

The same transformation had also overtaken the Sleeper. Gone was the elfin prince. The merest hint of tenderness and promise showed through the stony features of this sleeping giant. His massive limbs, formerly so ethereal, had become as rocklike as the couch on which he lay; and the half-raised hand, which had seemed to signal welcome and friendship, now jerked imperiously at its binding chain.

Outside, the birds were mobbing the summit of the Tower, their strident cries summoning Tom to the sun-lit world. But the child was equally demanding, groaning in its efforts to free itself and reach the Sleeper. Confused, Tom could not decide which way to turn – to the bright world of sea and sky or to the inner gloom of the chamber. He glanced questioningly at Blossom, but for the moment she appeared even less decided than he. She was looking distractedly about her, blinking away the last vestiges of her Dream-blindness. Unlike Tom, her Dream-damaged eyes had witnessed neither the depressing squalor of the settlement nor the crystal beauty of the Tower; and now, awake, she was not so much disappointed by this poorly-lit chamber as bewildered by it. Mystified to find it unchanged.

Her eyes settled at last on Tom's pack which showed as a ghostly hump set high on his shoulders. The sight of its dim outline seemed to steady her, to bolster some personal resolve. Her crippled body straightened slightly; her face took on the distant expression she might have shown to a stranger. Moving deliberately away from Tom, she placed herself between him and the nearest window. Then, pointing to the sleeping giant, she mouthed familiar words:

"You are the Carrier."

Familiar words, but spoken with a new authority, with a distinct air of challenge, as though she fully expected him to deny his Carrier role.

Hesitantly, under the watchful gaze of her dark untrusting eyes, he shrugged off the pack and took the naked body of the child in both hands. Here, in the hard physical world, it was a thing of light and shadow, with pale insubstantial limbs and hair as colourless and fine as gossamer. Although its eyes remained closed, it gave every other sign of wakefulness. Its tiny fists punched impatiently at the air; its face was screwed up in an anguish of anticipation; its toothless mouth gaped open as it let out sharp excited squeals.

"You are the Carrier," Blossom reminded him again,

renewing her challenge – her arms spread wide now, her body tense, ready to cut off his retreat should he try to reach the window.

Across her shoulder Tom could see bird-shapes fluttering in the window-space; hear shrill bird-cries vying with those of the child. And as hesitantly as before, willed on by Blossom's hardening resolve, he turned and approached the Sleeper.

With every dragging step he took, the huge figure showed more and more signs of life. The rocky limbs stirred, the dust of ages tumbling from them; the chest heaved, filling the chamber with the musty smell of stale air; the tempo of the twitching hand increased, jerking so hard at the chain that shards of rust sprang from the strained metal. Last of all, as Tom was about to deposit the squirming child in the Sleeper's lap, the flint-hard features of the face cracked and moved and the eyelids fluttered open. For a fraction of a second, that was all, yet long enough to reveal the eyes within.

Not the soft grey eyes of Tom's childhood memories. Not the eyes of the father he had lost and would never find again. These were a deep uncanny green; a green that knew nothing of sunlight and spring growth.

Tom's hands tightened about the child, drawing it back against his chest. While somewhere deep within him a familiar voice stirred into wakefulness as surely as did those limbs on the stone slab. A voice whose source he now knew for what it was. A thing as ancient and enduring as the Tower.

"Give the child up," it crooned. "Let the Dream have its way. Let it live again."

"Never . . . !" he tried to murmur, but no sound emerged.

The giant's eyelids fluttered open once more, as though sensing his reluctance, and suddenly the taloned bird-creature was glaring out at him. The face itself remained human in shape, but the eyes! They were the same fierce electric green as those he had glimpsed on the pinnacle, their elongated pupils flecked with furious red. They could have belonged only to a creature . . . no, a *force* that was as old as the

170

earth itself; and, like the earth, empty of all feeling. The Devil, his mother would have called it, but he knew better. There was no hatred or envy or pride in that baleful stare. Only a mindless hunger, a mindless will to survive. "No," he muttered.

It was the feeblest of protests, for still he was held by those twin slits of unholy green. Half mesmerised by them, he accepted at last where he had been in all his Dream ramblings. Into the frozen wastes of the past! Back into the dawn of human history! And beyond! To a time that knew nothing of love, nothing of gentleness, nothing of compassion. Where the heartless struggle for survival was all that mattered.

The shock of recognition made everything suddenly very clear to him. So the squalid settlement surrounding the icy tower *had* been real! And so had the barren wasteland through which he had journeyed. That was how the world had been in the long ago, which meant that all Mr Crawford's talk of a golden age had been nonsense. Little more than wishful thinking or childish make-believe. There had never been a golden age of peace and love; this town in which he had grown up had never been a place of "beauty and grace", "of ancient wisdom", as Mr Crawford had claimed. It had begun as a wretched cluster of hovels set in an ice-bound landscape; and its inhabitants, ground down by poverty and disease, had been ruled over by the Sleeper and his ancient bird-creature spirit. *That* was the truth behind Mr Crawford's fine words; that was the world he unwittingly yearned for. A world that would surely flourish again if ever the Sleeper and his ancient spirit were reunited.

Tom clutched the child more tightly still, mindful at last of what he had borne for so long: nothing less than the bird-creature itself, which he had surprised in its true form back there on the summit of the pinnacle. The child, in short, was the inhuman soul of this stony figure here before him; the Sleeper's secret identity no less, which had existed long before it had chosen to take on human form.

"No!" Tom repeated, far more forcefully than before

– denying those flickering eyelids; constraining the child as it struggled to break free.

The Tower responded to his denial by swaying alarmingly. The walls shook, shedding great clusters of salt crystal; the flagstoned floor creaked and groaned beneath his feet. With a clang, the chain binding the Sleeper snapped, and the huge fist groped blindly for him.

He leaped back, so eager to avoid those scrabbling fingers and flinty nails that he did not hear Blossom's light tread; he did not notice her stealing up beside him. Before he had sensed her nearness, she had snatched the child and darted off into the shadowy reaches of the chamber.

He recognised another harsh truth at that moment: that this was why she had accompanied him so far; why she had struggled through so many trials, driving her damaged body remorselessly. For this! So she could take over the role of Carrier should he fail at the end. From the very outset this had been her appointed task, her reason for remaining distant from him, for treating him so coolly.

But what of the trust and affection that had grown between them in recent days? Did that count for nothing? Even now he could read the conflict in her face. Doubt and affection warred there as she circled about him, trying to find a way past.

"We've made a mistake," he told her softly, blocking her path to the Sleeper at every turn. "We shouldn't be here. Everything Mr Crawford believed about the past is wrong. No one must wake the Sleeper. Ever! Look at his eyes and you'll see why."

She shook her head, suspecting a trick – the child, eyes still firmly closed, lying strangely still in her arms.

"It's all been a waste," he insisted, "the whole journey." She let out a whimper of denial, but he went on relentlessly, knowing that at this late stage he could not do other than hurt her. "Casey and the rest of them, they died for nothing. And so will you, so will we all, if . . ."

With a rush she was upon him, the child squirming

between them. She proved stronger and also wilier than he expected, almost slipping beneath his arms and ducking past. He forced her away, but she came at him again, rocking him backwards.

"You can't . . . !" he gasped, panting with the effort of fending her off. "What . . . Mr Crawford . . . told us . . . isn't true . . . The Sleeper's eyes . . . his eyes . . ."

She was no longer listening. She was fighting him in earnest now, defending not just the child, but her memory of Casey; pitting herself against Tom as she had pitted herself against the Tower, and with the same dogged persistence. He tried with all his might to push her away, but she pressed him so hard that despite his greater strength he was the one who steadily gave ground, stumbling nearer and nearer to the Sleeper's groping hand.

Once, and once only, those gnarled fingers grazed the back of his head. That icy touch had the same effect as before: it sent a shock of deep chill right through him, from his head down to the fossilized scale still hidden in his pocket.

The scale! He had all but forgotten it till then. An actual fragment of the past he feared! A part of the bird-creature, which stood now as proof of the creature's real-life existence; as an undeniable link between past and present, between Dream and reality.

That was exactly how Tom had thought of the scale when he had first prised it from its slab of flint: as a link between two orders of being. The memory of that evening came back to him even as he continued to struggle grimly with Blossom. Yes, the scale as a kind of link. And also, perhaps, as a means to power – power over the bird-creature which had produced it. Or so Tom had surmised up there on the fell in the falling dusk. Well, did the scale possess such power? Could it be used to bind the bird-creature to its pre-human past? To force it to reveal its true nature?

Tom could think of only one way of putting such questions to the test, and with a grunting effort he heaved Blossom from him and drew the scale hastily from his pocket. As she rushed forward yet again, he sidestepped and pressed the spangled shape onto the child's exposed thigh. It stuck fast to the ghostly flesh, a wisp of freezing vapour rising from the point of contact. There was a high squeal, as though the child had been scalded, and straight away the delicate eyelids flew open.

In that instant of exposure the elfin face lost all its elusive beauty, its once sensitive features disfigured by eyes that shone a lurid green. Not so much eyes any longer as two tunnels of poisoned light that glared out from emptiness. A similar disfigurement afflicted the tiny body as it rapidly took on the likeness of the bird-creature – the true spirit-self of the gigantic Sleeper. Its feet bunched into half-formed talons; the beginnings of a tail curled between its legs; its hands and arms were twisted into craggy pinions.

Blossom, horrified by what she found herself holding, snatched her hands away and let the creature drop to the floor. There, squirming and squealing, it completed its hideous transformation. Its thighs grew round and spangled, and its nose developed into a thrusting beak that struck at the dank stones of the floor in a desperate attempt to reach the Sleeper – to unite itself with the physical shape it had adopted here in the world of humankind. A union that would have woken the Sleeper from his age-long trance and brought the primitive horrors of the past alive once more, there in the dark tower's secret heart.

"Don't let them meet!" Tom yelled, and lunged forward.

Not for the first time, Blossom proved far quicker than he. Scooping up the wriggling shape, she ran with it to the window-space and tried to hurl it out into the void. It clung desperately to her, while the birds descended from every side, pecking and shrieking and beating at it with their wings.

Tom saw Blossom stagger drunkenly, jostled by hundreds of feathered bodies; saw her fling out her hands again and again in a futile attempt to dislodge what remained of the child. The creature merely gripped on more tightly, as if sensing that its fate was tied to hers.

She sensed it too, because she seemed to gather herself in the midst of the milling birds, to crouch and lean slightly forward as for a mighty leap.

"No!" Tom roared, and reached the window in time to catch her about the waist.

But as always there was a part of her he could not hold; that he could neither possess nor protect. Through a glare of sunlight he glimpsed her shadow-self – her Dream identity – as it leaped clear of her body and out into space, her ghostly hands still entwined with the talons of the bird-creature.

There was a pause, a dreadful emptiness, followed by the drawn-out cry of his own name, her voice filled with yearning as it broke free at last.

"T-o-o-o-m!"

Then she was gone. Lost in the crash of surf far below. Already the birds were drifting lazily away. The giant figure behind him had slumped back into its ageless sleep. And Tom? Blossom? They were left standing in the blind eye of the Tower, her empty body clasped closely in his arms.

20 Jack came to collect him in the early evening. He was sitting, as usual, beside Blossom's bed in the hospital, which was where he had spent most of the past week, watching her sink lower and lower. With the passage of the days her features had gradually lost their elfin quality and her face had returned to normal as she drifted from him.

"Any change?" Jack asked softly, and placed a comforting hand on his shoulder.

He shook his head, his gaze fixed unwaveringly on her closed eyelids.

Jack stood beside him, contemplating the shadowy hollows of her face which had deepened even since his visit on the previous evening. Her breath, now, was so light and quick that the sheet covering her body barely moved.

"She'll be leaving us soon," he said gently. "Like all the others. You might as well admit it. Her spirit's adrift somewhere. And when the spirit's lost and gone, the body must soon follow. That's how it is."

Tom's only answer was to reach for her hand which lay placidly on the coverlet, her fingers as pale as the surrounding walls.

"She's had enough of this," Jack whispered. "We all have. She'll be better off out of it. She served her turn at the end, and she did it with honour. That's as much as any of us can ask for."

When Tom did not answer, Jack bent over him, almost fatherly in his concern, his blue eyes clouding to grey in the poorly lit ward.

"I can guess how you feel, lad," he murmured, "but all your tears won't keep her here. Let her go. It's what she'd want for herself. Also it's the right thing to do, and the fair."

Reluctantly, Tom released her hand and allowed himself to be led down the length of the ward, though his eyes lingered on her face until the very last moment.

In silence they entered the darkened street together. Heads bowed, their booted feet ringing on the cobblestones, they paced slowly from one pool of lamplight to the next, following the string of modern electric lights that wound up through the old hilltown.

Outside Tom's house they stood for a while and surveyed the scene beneath them. Much of the town's ugliness was hidden by darkness; but so too was the natural beauty of its setting. In the absence of a moon, sea and sky merged into a single bowl of night, so black that not even Tower Rock showed against it. They could sense the Rock there, however, hard and obdurate, an intrusion from another age. As if in defiance of its presence, a train hooted somewhere in the valley; and over by the mill a ragged flame punctured the dark and subsided. Much closer to where they stood, the night was alive with small homely sounds. The closing of a door; a jingle of song from a shopfront tavern; the barking of a dog, dull and monotonous.

"It's not much," Jack muttered half to himself, "but it's a sight better than what used to be here – than the old world Crawford pined for. And it'll get better yet with any luck. Not for everyone maybe, but for most."

"You think so?" Tom asked.

"That's my hope anyway."

"But doesn't that make you a bit like Mr Crawford?" Tom objected. "A golden future – a golden past – they sound the same to me. The same mistake all over again, except in reverse. I'll take the present and leave you and Crawford to quarrel over the past and future."

Jack chuckled softly. "You may be right, lad, but then I'm not looking for any golden time to come. A small improvement, that'll be enough. Even a half-step

177

forward is worthwhile if it takes us further from the Sleeper."

The mention of the Sleeper served as a reminder of what still lay in store for them, and they turned to face each other. Not as close friends – they would never be that – but as people with a mutual respect.

"Will tonight finish it?" Tom asked.

Jack nodded. "I expect so. After that it'll be all over for us. We'll have done our duty the way Blossom did hers. And the Tower will be for other generations to deal with. Other misguided fools like Crawford, and other hearts as true as yours and Blossom's at the end."

With that closing remark they parted – Jack striding off down the street; Tom entering his home where his mother and Denny were waiting anxiously.

He paused briefly at the foot of the stairs. "This'll be the last time, Ma," he told her, and saw relief flood into her face.

"Then take especial care," she said. "There are too many grieving households in this town already."

And from Denny, his shrill voice following Tom up the stairwell: "Don't stay there, Tom. Make sure you come back to us."

Denny's words recurred to him minutes later, when he lay down on his bed, except that now they had little to do with thoughts of his own safety. He repeated them drowsily, pleading with the darkness and with Blossom's lost spirit as he drifted off to sleep.

"... come back ... Don't stay ... not there ... there ..."

... there was the portal. An oval of grey light set against a black screen. As he stepped up to it and through, out into a wintry overcast day, he detected Blossom's ghostly presence close beside him, more faded and insubstantial than when he had last left her. He turned, but she had flitted off into a faint drift of mist, her footsteps so feather-soft that they made no impress in the snow.

He was left standing in a vaguely familiar valley, its floor strewn with icy boulders, its sides rising vertically to form sheer cliffs. Over near the far cliff he could see Jack waiting patiently – a figure as familiar as the valley – and he trudged through the snow to join him.

"All's well," Jack said, and nodded towards a sledge parked beneath an overhang of the cliff.

Bound to it with glistening thongs was the spirit of the Sleeper. Ever since the fall from the Tower, it had abandoned the form of child or bird-creature and reverted to its other shape: that of the old man whom Tom had first encountered in the icy room right back at the start of the Dream journey.

As on that distant occasion, his withered limbs lay deathly still; his parchment-like skin was stained bluish-grey by the cold and covered with a glitter of frost. He had lain like that, unmoving on the sledge, throughout their long trip from the crystal tower, never once showing any sign of life.

"Do you think he's dead?" Tom asked – too loudly, because the word "dead" echoed from cliff to cliff like booming laughter.

Jack shook his head and handed Tom the second of the two harnesses attached to the sledge. "The Sleeper never dies," he answered softly, as though ensuring that the bound and frozen figure should not hear. "Like the earth itself, like the Tower in which he lies bound, he's always with us, waiting for us to relax our guard."

Tom knew with one part of his mind that what Jack said was true. Yet all at once, there in the grey calm of the morning, he found it hard to believe. The old man – the Sleeper's spirit-self – seemed too dormant, too weathered by the years, to offer any further threat. Banished once more, his life, his power, had surely been extinguished forever. It was too late for him to be re-united with the Sleeper ever again. Death had sundered them. Or so the inner voice suggested, whispering to Tom so subtly and insistently that he could not distinguish its low murmur from the flow of his own thoughts or from the mutter of the wind as it blew sluggishly along the valley. "Dead," the voice suggested, giving him back the echo of his earlier utterance. "Dead." Repeating the word until it was scored into his consciousness.

He did not tell Jack of his new-found conviction, wary still of those hard blue eyes. At the prompting of the voice, he preferred to keep the secret of the old man's death to himself. Dutifully, giving no outward sign of disagreement, he donned

179

the harness and secured it across his chest. Then, with Jack beside him, he leaned against the inertia of the sledge and set off on the last stage of their journey.

Despite the desolation of the valley, they did not travel alone. Always, whenever Tom raised his head, Blossom's shadowy presence was there with them, following their winding progress along the valley floor. He glimpsed rather than actually saw her: the merest outline of a person who dissolved into the flat white background the moment he tried to bring her into sharp focus.

She, too, the voice dismissed. "An illusion," it whispered, planting the seed of doubt in his mind. "A will-o'-the-wisp. Nothing more." And later, when the ghost of a loved face flashed across his vision: "Just a flurry of snow raised by the wind. That's all." Hour by hour the voice droned on, impressing upon him the emptiness, the deathliness of this wasteland, until by early evening he had ceased to glance around at any hint of movement, his eyes fixed on the snow that passed beneath his feet. Now, if any other voice called faintly to him, he failed to hear it, deaf to all but the voice within.

Long shadows streaked the valley when they finally stopped.

"It's time, lad, time!" Jack was shouting – meaningless words that came crashing through the murmurous silence.

Stiff and numb from cold, he raised his eyes towards a known expanse of cliff. Half way up its face, and set back from a narrow ledge, he could make out a darkened doorway, its lintel strung with the shattered remains of icicles. Yes, he thought dully, that's the place. Slipping off his harness he reached for the rope which Jack had already attached to the sledge . . . and all at once she was there again, standing between him and the cliff, barring his way.

He hesitated, and Jack pulled him back. "No, lad," he said firmly. "You've done your share of dangerous climbs. This is for me to do."

The voice, however, believed otherwise. "You are the Carrier," it reminded him. "You alone. No one else."

It was true. Or at least it seemed to be in the hazy light of evening, with heavy dusk encroaching across the valley floor. A half memory came back to him, of a long successful climb,

180

to a dark eyrie in the sky. Hadn't that earned him the right to this final task? Hadn't it?

Unsure, he closed his ears to everything but the voice. To its soothing confidence which banished all uncertainty and grief.

"You cannot fail us," it instructed him. Then, in a pleading tone: "Do it for me. I beg of you." Speaking to him now from the sunken mouth of the old man. A dying request which he could not refuse.

Moved by pity, he snatched the rope from Jack's hands and ran for the cliff. Her frail presence still hovered in his path, but blind to everything except the old man's need he swept her aside. With a swiftness that neither she nor Jack could match, he began the climb, his rapid ascent outstripping the advancing shadows.

He had almost reached the ledge, the open doorway only a metre or two above his head, when the change came. A breath of burning wind that issued from the old man's sunken mouth – from the hideous spirit of the Sleeper that had tricked him yet again and was now taking its revenge. Instantly, under the pressure of that hot wind, the valley floor melted and turned into a churning river dotted with icefloes. He glanced down, in time to see the sledge and its hoary burden sink beneath the surface, the attached rope snapping tight and nearly dragging him from the cliff. There was a low chuckle, the voice no longer pretending to be other than it was. "Come to me," it whispered mockingly, and the weight of the sledge increased, pulling so hard that all he could do was close his eyes and hold on, the rope biting into his stomach.

"Cut the rope!" Jack yelled, swarming up to help him. "Cut it!"

How could he? He had no knife. And even to have released one hand would have meant disaster.

" I can't!" he sang out, aware that he could not possibly hang on long enough for Jack to reach him.

Which left only Blossom. Bird-like, she rose to meet him. Even without turning his head he could sense her there. Her eyes darker than the twilight. Her hands fluttering like pale doves in the falling dusk as they settled on the rope and eased the weight.

"Now . . ." she sighed, a living breath that brought with it the fresh scent of heather from the fell. "Now . . ."

For a few seconds she bore the full weight of the sledge. Enough time for him to slip the rope. To clutch again at the cliff-face. Safe! Sobbing with relief. So thankful that he barely registered her passing. A feather-touch of lips was all he felt. And when he turned, expecting still to find her there, the evening was strangely empty. Only he and Jack were left clinging to the cliff. Far below, where the river had magically re-frozen, the greenish outline of the Sleeper's ancient spirit (part man, part bird-creature, part child) shone dimly through the ice, his ancient form locked now in the wasteland's wintry heart.

There was a momentary pause, a mere catch of the breath, as Tom searched the gathering dusk in vain. Then, with the long shadows of night creeping up the cliff to envelop him, he threw back his head and called aloud her name as she had once called his. A wrenching cry, of unbearable loss and longing, that split the starless heavens and freed him at last from the toils of the Dream.

An Afterword

He never married; and during a long life spent working the cliffs, he never fell. In his middle years he inherited Jack's position as foreman of the climbers, though never once was he called upon to act with Jack's sternness. Other young hopefuls lifted their eyes to the blind summit of Tower Rock, but always a kindly word of warning was enough to deter them, coming as it did from the one man reputed to have scaled the Rock and survived.

In the course of time the town changed just as Jack had hoped it might. The mill and the mine closed down, replaced by a number of gentler industries; and where once the poor had trudged the cobbled streets, now those streets were explored by eager-eyed tourists who exclaimed over the quaintness of the old houses.

Those same tourists, in their shiny cars, also lined the cliffs to watch the antics of the birds and the daring feats of the fabled climbers. If they were lucky, they even caught a glimpse of the most famous climber of them all.

An old man now, he left the safety of beach or clifftop only once a year. At the start of spring. In order to scale the spire and greet the incoming birds. Perched high on a weathered ledge, with Tower Rock at his back, he opened his arms to the feathered shapes that came skimming across the emptiness of sea and sky towards him. For a few minutes only, as they circled about his head, he was transported back to the far-off days of his youth. Briefly the pressure of their milling bodies conjured for him the boisterous energy of a long-lost friend Their high-pitched cries, strangely song-like, stirred memories of once faithful companions. But most of all the spring-time presence of the birds reminded him of someone especially dear. Someone who, as her name suggested, had fallen early and left him alone there on the heights. Eyes closed in that first moment of greeting, he forgot about Tower Rock, banished it to the dark spaces of his mind. His cheeks and lips caressed by the feather-touch of wings, he searched for and found her again. Held her there just long enough to express, through the simple gesture of his upflung arms, all that world of feeling he had never expressed in words.